Printed in Canada

Published by Lulu in; 2014

www.lulu.com

Godard, Hannah J. 2000

For the Beautiful People

Hannah Joy Godard

ISBN: 978-1-312-43463-9

First edition
Written by Hannah Godard
Illustrations by Kyra Yeske

Enjoy the illustrations!.
KuYeske

To Emily, to show you that life does go on. And everything will work itself out.

HAPPY READING!.

Thank you

FOR THE
BEAUTIFUL
PEOPLE

6

Chapter 1

Being different is not necessarily bad. Being different makes you special, it makes you desirable and unique. Sometimes people want to be different but they don't know how to do it. They want to be special and unique, which they are, it's not a put-down, everyone is special. They just can't see how special they are. That's why they put-down the different ones. They don't want them to feel the way they want to feel, like they are special and extraordinary. These ones are the beautiful people, the gems of the world. But you would never know because they are the ones that hide, the ones that are made fun of.

My name is Adeline. I live with my parents in a small home. They are both accountants. I go to school at TR Treyton.

8

—*σπεχιαλ*—

My school is small but has many kids in it. I am one of the outcasts, one of the outsiders. I don't have a group of friends to fit in with.

One group of kids target me. They push me into the corner and throw my books. I wait for them to pass and then collect my things and run to my next class. They pull my hair and call me names but I can't do anything about it. It's not a fair fight, three to one, and I wouldn't stand a chance. I could say that everyone else is innocent but they see it happening and don't do anything. That's just like doing it to me yourself.

So now instead of being part of the kids, in their groups and play dates, I'm just part of the school - a fly on the wall. I observe everyone and study their behaviour. During lunch I watch in the halls. That's my life, and that's how I will live it.

I have always been good at school. I was never top of the class but made my parents proud with a steady stream of A's and B's. Every term we have a class election to see who will be president of the class. They have many jobs to fill which, to a twelve year old, seems like the best news in the world. The jobs include: bringing down the attendance; assigning the weekly jobs; organizing each week's gratitude circle, which consists of saying three things you are grateful for and then receiving a treat of some kind (most of the time it was gummy worms); and last but not least, being in charge when the teacher is gone. This was the most appealing to a bunch of twelve year olds who, until that moment, didn't have much power or say over anything.

We are only allowed to have four people campaign, so the first four to sign up get the job. This is where my story begins. In grade seven.

—υνιθυε—

Today is the day of my big election. My friends are supposed to meet me outside of the school so we can walk in together as one big political party.

My favourite part of being class president (if I get elected of course,) is being able to take the attendance down. The ladies at the front office always have nice candy. I only like the first one though; the one at the back is always grumpy and yells at me for whatever I do.

My mom pulls our car into the parking lot of our small school which is only about 300 kids. It goes from grade one to nine but there is only one class for each grade.

I see my friends waiting outside the doors of the school and quickly turn to my mom and give her a kiss before hopping out of the car and running over to my friends.

"Hi," I say as I approach them.

"Hey! Today is the big day!" says Payton. She is also running in the election but we decided that we would co-run the class if either of us got elected.

"I'm kind of nervous but I'm also really excited!" I reply.

"Don't worry! I bet we'll both do great. Hey, I gotta go talk to Alyssa about the clothes I lent her," says Payton.

"OK, I'll just wait here."

I watch as my other two friends, Kaitlyn and Elisha, scurry off behind her.

A sudden chill comes on and I decide to go inside and set up my things before the big election, which will be held in advisory.

My grade seven class is right next to the front office so I don't have to walk very far.

The school is very old and the door makes a faint creaking sound as I push it open. Mr. Dunval isn't in the class yet so I set my books down and wait patiently at my desk.

Soon, more kids flood into the class and eventually so does Mr. Dunval. Payton sits at the back of the class and I'm at the front. Elisha and Kaitlyn are side by side on the left side of the room.

"Welcome back, everyone. As you all must know, today is a big day. Now I would like to share with you the results of the election you did on Friday. I would like to also congratulate all the applicants. There was only a two vote difference between first and second. Would you like me to read the results fourth to first or first to fourth?"

"Fourth to first!" the class cries out.

I really don't care as long as we get to first at some point.

"Ok. In fourth place is Dylan."

Everyone turns to Dylan who lets out a small laugh. He was probably just in it for the laughs anyway.

"In third place is Sophia. And in second place is... drum roll please."

The class all hits their legs and some boys hit their stomachs. It's only between me and Payton now.

"In second place is Payton. Congratulations Adeline on being the new class president for this term!"

Everyone claps and I take a quick peak at Payton. Her eyes are angry and her cheeks are red. She avoids my gaze and stares right where Mr. Dunval used to be standing.

The bell rings and the students file out of the class, heading towards their next period class. As I'm walking out the door I feel something come hard against my leg and I lose my balance, falling to the floor. A face emerges on top of me.

"Freak," Payton says before following the class out the door with Elisha and Kaitlyn following her like lost puppies.

Stunned, I pick myself up off the ground and find my way out of the class. Everything happened so fast I can't understand. All through Math and Science I have to sit alone.

I don't understand at all, anything. Everything is turned upside down and I can't find my way back. But I can't tell her that. I have to pick myself up and keep moving forward.

"Welcome class," Mrs. Smith says as she enters the class. She teaches me Science, one of my favourite subjects.

Everyone stays in their places without saying anything. I know why. Today we get to dissect lamb hearts. Fun.

"Now, you all know what to do, we talked about this yesterday. Get in your groups and come grab a heart."

Unfortunately, me and Payton are together. I scurry up and grab one of the small, blue hearts. For some reason, all the hearts are pink and blue and purple. I have no idea why but it looks like someone strangled them and they turned blue.

Payton is positioned at the table where we have to start our dissection. I walk over and set the heart on the table.

"Are you ready? I'll get the camera ready since we have to video it." I say.

Payton just sits there and picks at the purple nail polish painted over her almond shaped nails. I set the camera down on the table and press play. I wait for Payton to start her part like we practiced yesterday but she just sits there so I step in, saying both of our lines. She doesn't even touch her knife.

I poke and prod at the heart, explaining what each little blue discoloured piece is while she sits there. Within minutes I have found every piece on our checklist and our heart looks like an animal tried to eat it but gave up, then put it in the middle of the road and it was hit by a transport truck thirty six times, and then went through a wood chipper.

I can't believe her. But she's just sad she didn't win. I have to cut her some slack since she's hurting. She would do the same for me, so I clean up and hand in our camera with our video without reporting Payton.

"Great job today, guys. I'll be watching your videos tonight. Now, since you did so well, I guess you can go early. See you tomorrow."

Everyone cheers and gets up and out quickly in case she changes her mind. I grab my binder from under my desk and head out of the class. We've got French next and that's Payton's least favourite class so I don't think I'll try to talk to her when she's already in a bad mood.

I quickly slide the books into my locker and reach for my French binder. While I'm reaching for it I feel something hard brush past me, pushing me into my locker. My hands land hard onto of my dividers but luckily they stop me and I don't fall onto the floor.

—σπεχιαλ—

Now the whole class is staring at me. They all heard the rumours that I cheated - that I came in early and added more votes. Of course, I did come in early - I was the first in the class. The only one that saw me was Sophia, but she is too scared to say anything.

Finally, lunch is here. I normally sit with Payton but I guess that can't happen today. I don't know where I should sit so I walk into the cafeteria alone.

The cafeteria is small but is set up with rows of tables. The café is on the far side. Every day there is a different special and all the specials are included with our tuition. You can also buy other things like donuts and brownies and PowerAde but you have to pay for those.

Nobody looks at me. They are all caught up in their conversations. They don't even glance my way. All they do is keep on moving. Besides, nothing's wrong in their world. In fact, nothing could be better.

I see Payton at the café and I decide to walk up. She can't be angry with me forever. I don't even know what I did.

"Hey", I say as I approach her. She doesn't turn back to look at me. Neither do Elisha and Kaitlyn.

I walk up beside her and take my tray from the stack. I push it along the rolling bars, collecting my portions of today's special which happens to be beef on a bun with veggies and choice of sauce. Payton's favourite.

"Which sauce are you choosing?" I ask Payton, trying to make conversation. I'm trying to overlook what she did to me: tripping me, calling me a freak. She was hurt she didn't win. I can't blame her.

I don't know what else to say. Me talking is making Kaitlyn and Elisha look uncomfortable but they never did talk much. They keep looking down and I don't want to make them feel uncomfortable. Besides, it's not their fault.

I finally reach the end of the line where we pick up our beef. I can smell the sauce from behind Payton and I realize how hungry I really am. And then, an idea hits me; my last hope to make it all better again.

"I know this is your favourite. You could have mine," I say. Bribery is my last hope.

All of a sudden, Payton spins around and throws her tray of food on me.

"Not anymore."

Her hands feel cold on my open shoulder as she pushes me down to the ground. People turn to look at us and she bends down and lies beside me like she slipped.

"Leave us alone, freak. Leave me alone. You are alone. Forget about me. And them. Forget about everyone. Just..." she pauses before continuing, looking me right in the eye, "...disappear."

"Are you ok?" someone asks us.

Before I have time to answer, Payton jumps in and replies "Yeah, we're fine. She just slipped and sprayed her food, caught my foot going down and we both went."

"You both should get to the bathroom, maybe call home and get some clothes."

"No, no. We're fine." Payton says.

Then the girl turns to me. "Adeline, you should at least go to the bathroom and wash up. You've got food all over yourself."

"Yeah, maybe I should," I say slowly, still trying to take in what happened.

"Do you want one of us to come with you?" she asks me.

"No, that's ok. I think I'll be fine."

"Ok, maybe you could just change into your gym strip if you can't get all the food out. You're going to start smelling like beef on a bun soon," she says and everyone laughs, including Payton.

Great. Just another thing for Payton to make fun of. This day just keeps getting better and better.

Before I leave I take a look at Payton. She's staring at me. The people are starting to clear but she stays put. Even when I turn around I can feel her gaze burning through my clothes. This isn't over. And it never will be.

Chapter 2

So that's my back story. That is how I ended up here. See how just the smallest things can set people off?

I am now going into grade nine. This all started in September of grade seven and now I am in grade nine. I had to survive all of grade seven and eight with Payton taking every opportunity she had to make me feel smaller and break my heart more than it already was.

Today is just one more day in a series of days. One day of three hundred and sixty five days. I got to school extra early today but not early enough. When I walked through the big front doors where I once stood talking to Payton, the other kids were already there and hustling through the halls.

Sometimes I think I am invisible. I get pushed and shoved in the halls and no one seems to notice - except for Payton who takes pleasure in it. But I can't really do anything about it because I have no one to stand up for me. No one to back me up. So I just have to put up with it and try to ignore it - to forgive and move on.

Kaitlyn and Elisha have started to be part in Payton's bullying. But still, Payton is the ring leader. Her attention has somewhat shifted from me to everyone. I guess after she started bullying me she realized that she was actually quite good at it and took to making everyone around her feel bad. I don't think people notice or maybe they just don't care because somehow she's part of the "popular people."

The only people she can't bully are Rachel, Tanison, Tasha, and Emily. They are too confident to get bullied by Payton.

Even though I am confident in my abilities, I don't have a group of friends to back me up. Maybe their hate just cuts a little deeper on me since they were my friends. It stings like your parents abandoning you. No matter how many friends you have, you will never feel as loved as you would by your own parents.

I am suddenly shaken from the dream state that I am in. I see Payton out of the corner of my eye and can feel her eyes lock on me... the same kind of burning sensation as before. I can hear her walking faster towards me. I try to walk faster but I am stuck behind everyone. She walks up and is now directly behind me. All she does is stand there.

I continue to walk behind the crowd, keeping my muscles tight. Payton begins to step on the back of my heels. At first I thought it was by accident but then it picked up. Now every footstep is a sharp pain in my heels. I let out a small scream that can barely be heard over the sound of the other kids in the halls.

"Stop," I finally squeak out.

"Why? Who's going to make me?" she replies.

"Stop!" I scream, still not loud enough to be heard by anyone else. This time sounded more like a cry and I immediately wish I could take it back.

"Oh baby! You can cry in here." She pushes me into the open janitor's closet and closes the door.

The cement floor is cold but I don't feel like getting up. All I want to do is sit here and wait. Wait until someone comes or I hear the bell. I'll be OK in here anyway.

I pull out my iPod, the only thing I bring to school that's important but not too devastating to be "lost" or in other words stolen by Payton. I turn on Kelly Clarkson's song "People Like Us."

This song helps me when I feel like my life is over. I need to remind myself that my life has just started and I'm too young to write off my life. The people like us, we've got to stick together.

The song finishes, I get up and walk out. Head held high. Crisis averted.

—υνιθυε—

Very boring day. Like all days. Three hundred and sixty five days a year. Sit alone. Think alone. Be alone. But rule number one; don't let it get you down.

I have now created a process for lunches. I walk in and get my food. I then sit in a small area, maybe meant for a garbage can or something. There, squished between three walls, I will eat. The best part about this spot is that I can see and observe everyone. And that is what I do.

I pull out my iPod and video every table. Starting at the small round tables where grades one to five sit.

They look care-free. They are friends with everyone and everything comes easy to them.

Next I focus on my grade. The people I like to video the most are Rachel and Tasha. They seem nice but they never let anyone sit with them. They laugh and talk but they never accept anyone. Rachel is a dancer. You can see that just by the way she walks. Tasha is a volleyball player, Tanison is a hockey player, and Emily plays ringette.

Then there's Payton's "group." They always fight amongst themselves and are hated by everyone. They don't seem to care though. They do their hair and makeup and everyone seems to suck up to them but at the same time, everyone hates them. Elisha and Kaitlyn follow Payton around like lost puppies and the two new girls, Nicole and Ashley, seem to just twirl their hair and avoid the mud. It's funny to watch them. All they do is stand around a bench and talk during lunch. I now forever associate the sound of clicking high heels on the floor with them. I never knew it was possible to wear a dress during the winter but apparently when you want something desperately you can find a way to do it. No matter how stupid it is.

When the bell rings, I stay put and wait for all the kids to file out and then slowly follow behind them. Now we have free time which used to mean we had to go outside but now means we can just go wherever we want.

I decide to sit in the closet I was in this morning. It wasn't too bad. I have been trying to start a video blog with all my video I have been taking. I find them quite interesting and I think other people might too. I open the MG Movies app on my small iPod screen. I first have to upload all the videos I just took which normally takes forever.

I watch as the numbers flash by on the screen and the videos drop, one by one, into the box on the screen. I organize all the videos in order so they make sense, organizing the grade one to five separate from the nines and those are separate from the eights and so on.

That's all I have time for before the loud bell rings. There must be a speaker in here because it's louder than outside.

If I hurry I can get to class before the mob of people come.

I make it to class in record time and take my seat. There are only two more periods and then I can go home and edit my film.

—σπεχιαλ—

The rest of the day was uneventful as always and so was the car ride home. I answered the usual questions: how was your day? what did you do? My parents seemed to have stopped asking if I was OK and if Payton finally forgave me. And I have stopped answering.

As soon as I enter the door I run to my room and sit down at my desk.

My room is small but has a very nice circular window with a bench underneath. I like this because I can look out into the yard and watch the kids next door playing. This might sound very stalker-ish but if you haven't had a friend come over in three years then it's nice to see other people having fun.

Now I add music and transitions and words to my video. This doesn't take very long, but it's my favourite part. Since I'm making it on MG Movies I can work on it on my iPod and my computer.

I chose the song "People Like Us" because I use it for everything. And it was also one of the few songs on my iPod.

I finished just in time to go down for dinner. Tonight we're having meatballs and salad which is not particularly my favourite but I'm so hungry I don't really care. I didn't eat anything at lunch because I was too busy filming.

"How was your day?" my dad asks me as I sit down at the dinner table. Mom drove me home from school so it's his turn to ask.

"It was ok I guess," I answer. I am tired of answering these questions.

"What did you do?"

"Nothing much."

The silence that follows is more awkward than the questions so I decide to fill it in.

"How was your day?" I ask him.

"It was average. I had a very long meeting. The project manager wanted to collect the data for our new project which was something I wasn't in charge of, but he asked me to do that anyway so I told him..." I stopped listening.

Everything is the same over and over again.

Chapter 3

I am walking through the school. The halls are all empty. I can't see anyone and I can't hear anyone. Everything is blurry. I am looking at the walls, at the lockers. Everything looks fine. I round a corner and everyone is standing along the side of the walls. It's like I walked into a normal day. They are all chatting and laughing.

Suddenly, they all stop and look at me. I am alone; no one is standing beside me. Everyone is quiet as I walk towards the end of the hall. They all stare at me. I can feel their eyes burning through my clothes.

I start to run and they all chase me. I run towards my room. I drop all my books on the ground and run as fast as I can. I can hear their footsteps coming behind me, faster and faster.

I reach the door of my room and turn the knob but it won't budge. I shake it and bang on the door but it won't open. They are halfway down the hall so I try to run but my feet are stuck. I can't move and I can't talk. I try to scream and yell but no sound will come out.

Finally I give up and curl up in a ball. I bang my fist on the ground trying to get them to go away. I open my mouth to scream and this time sound does come out.

—υνιθυε—

I wake with a start. My whole body is shaking and covered in sweat. I place my hand on my heart to try to slow my heart beat. It was just a dream. Just a dream.

Chapter 4

I have decided to start driving to school extra early so I can skip the rush of kids and most importantly, Payton. If I get to school before the rest of the people, then I can get to class extra early, take my seat and disappear from the sight of all the people who might make me a target. I think this would be best for me. But obviously my mom doesn't know that's why I'm doing this. She just thinks that I have school work I need to catch up on.

My mom drives me to school and drops me off right in front of the school. Not a single bus in sight. Just the way I like it. There are only two cars in the parking lot in front of the school, one for Mrs. Price and another for Mr. Stewart, the principals.

"Ok. See you tonight," I say to my mom before she drives away.

"Goodbye, sweetie. I love you."

"Love you too." I lean through the window and give her a quick kiss.

I wish I could stay home, maybe be home schooled, but my parents are too busy to home school me and where would just not going get me? I would have to live at home forever. I would rather suffer through the next three years than waste my life just because of one person.

No one has gotten to the school yet so I can finally walk down the hallways without being scared, without needing to hide. The hallways creak under the weight of my body. Every footstep can be heard in the empty hallways.

I find my locker, put my things away, and then hurry off to class. My locker always used to be clean and tidy but in the last few years I have just been throwing my books in and taking my other books out since I have to hide from Payton.

The door of the class is next to my locker, a spot I specifically chose so I can spend as little time as possible in the halls.

And then I wait. I look ahead, to the boards, and wait. And wait. The first bell goes. The second bell goes. People start filling in and I just wait, not moving.

—σπεχιαλ—

The bell rings, loud and clear. People start to file out of the class the same way that they came in. Like mindless clones, they always walk the same. Laughing and talking.

I walk into the halls after everyone has come out of the class. People are sitting in the halls eating and laughing together. At break, all the people have to eat in the halls but at lunch we can go wherever we want. Most people eat in the cafeteria. I can't sit in the halls without being pushed or made fun of. That's why I sit in "The Room".

This is actually a long story but to tell the story of my life I have to add in this part.

—υνιθυε—

I was walking through the school, going to get paper for one of my projects and I saw Payton. I could hear her a mile away, the click click click of her high heels.

I can't run. I can't hide. I just continue to walk. I soon reach the end of the hallway with Payton on my heels.

"Where are you going? Where are you going to hide?" I hear her ask, her voice like ice, chilling me to the bone.

I keep walking. I don't look back. I see a door at the end of the hall. It's unlocked and open just a crack. As I approach I dive into the room and close the doors. Out of the corner of my eye, as I am diving into the room, I see Payton walk into the paper room.

Instead of leaving the room I look around. There is a bench at the end of the room, in front of a long line of windows. There are small cabinets holding paint and paper. The floor is blue tile and the walls are white. There is the odour of freshly sharpened pencils in the air that makes it smell like the place I hate but it is also soothing.

I grab a sheet of paper from my newly found room and head back to class.

I have spent the rest of my lunch hours in that room, the room I hide in.

—σπεχιαλ—

So I sit in the closet and look out the windows. For so long I have hated this place but now I found this room and I finally have something to look forward to. I have always thought that there would be something to look forward to, that there must be something good, you just have to look.

After I finish eating my lunch I go back to the corner where I sat to film. I mostly film Rachel and Tasha. They are the most interesting. I have enough of Payton talking and gossiping. I like to find new things to film.

Rachel is a dancer and acts like a dancer. She is sweet and kind but knows that she's beautiful and doesn't need to be told it. Sometimes she can be a little too cocky but most of the time she is sweet.

Tasha knows she is the best and never lets anyone forget it. She can be careless and rude but she can also be sweet. She knows that she is popular and most of the time she doesn't care for the people below her.

Tanison is sporty, and she's popular. She doesn't care for anyone but the people in her group and she won't let anyone else in. She judges you before she knows you but when she gets to like you, she can be sweet and caring.

Emily is short but doesn't let that get in her way. She loves to play sports but knows she isn't good at all of them. She is always sweet. She lets everyone in and talks to everyone. She never judges anyone. I can see her friends pushing her away, replacing her, and I feel bad. People have come and gone from that group but Emily has been there since the start, and now she is being pushed out.

Out of the corner of the camera, I can see another girl who is out of place in the cafeteria. She has short brown hair and blue eyes. She is wearing a short purple skirt and a long sleeve, blue shirt that is tucked into her skirt. The moment that I first saw her I recognize her. She has Down's Syndrome. Normally the special needs kids eat in room 10 and that is also where they take all their classes so I don't know her too well. I also don't know why she is here. Normally they don't interact with us because they might have an attack or make a scene and upset all the other kids.

I am quick to forget her and the only thing reminding me of her presence in the cafeteria that day was the footage I caught of her. And even in that, she is in the bottom corner.

Chapter 5

I think. I can't breathe. I can't see.

I have a dreamless sleep tonight. Thoughts pop in and out of my head. They don't form into anything, they just stay like individual blobs, floating around in my head.

I think about Payton. How much I hate her. How she hurts me. I really just wish she would let me be. I want to be left alone. I wouldn't have any problems if she just left me alone.

I think about my parents. How I know that this is hurting them too but I can't stop it. I have tried to lie to them, to make it easier, but I just can't seem to get them to believe me. I want to be able to tell them that everything is ok, but that would be lying.

I think about that girl, the one in my footage. I think about how her life is. What she does every day. How she goes about living. I don't know why I wonder about her but I do. I just can't help it.

I don't sleep well. I toss and turn trying to shake my thoughts.

Chapter 6

My mom normally drives me home from school but today I decide I will walk. It is nice out for fall and I didn't even have to wear my coat.

The walk home is very long and uneventful. The path takes me around the river and is shaded with trees. The leaves were slowly floating off their branches and covering me as if to shade me from the outside world. All I can hear is the soothing sound of my footsteps and the slow rhythm of my heart beating in my chest. Thump, thump, thump.

My house is one of many in my suburb. All the houses look alike, small and white, with black roofs and small sidewalks leading up to them. My house, however, is smaller than the rest. It has a beat-up minivan parked out front and a very small back yard. Our front yard is non-existent.

Even though the outside is ordinary, the inside is quite cozy. The front door leads into the kitchen, which is small but looks huge because of the open concept. On the other side of the room is a sun porch that is made of glass. There are three steps leading down to the living room, which consists of a TV, a couch, three chairs and a giant cabinet, holding games.

If you keep walking down the hall there is my bedroom and my bathroom. The only way to get to the bathroom is through my bedroom.

My room is small. The best part about it is the one wall that is shaped like a circle and full of windows. I can look over the hill and down to the lake. Along the wall with windows I have a bench that follows the wall and stops when the windows stop. Does this remind you of something? My bedroom looks exactly like the room I found in school, with the windows and cabinets. In my room though, instead of being filled with paper and paint, my cabinets are filled with knick-knacks, clothes and toys. Most of my toys consist of board games. My bed is pushed up against the wall and the foot of my bed touches the wall right of the door. On the opposite side of the room is my bathroom. It's small but has a shower, a sink and a toilet.

In my favourite spot on that window I cut out part of the bench so I can fit my desk and my computer. Now while I work on my video I can look out onto the lake. I have to say, this is my favourite room in the house.

I open the video I started working on at lunch and continue to organize the videos, add music, scene changes and all sorts of effects. It's much easier on the computer than on my small iPod screen.

Once my video is finished, I upload the first day to YouTube. I have had this channel for a while but have never had anything to put on it. Now that I have these videos, I can finally upload them and maybe get some hits.

My channel name is Kendal Cook so no one will know it is me. For good or for bad, the only person that will know is me.

"Dinner Adeline!" I hear my mother yell from the kitchen.

"What is it?" I yell back.

"Doesn't matter. You've got to come anyway," she replies.

That answer normally means something I don't like.

I let out a small groan and then make my way to the kitchen. As I approach I can smell broccoli and tuna salad - my least favourite foods.

I sit down at the small, circular table and watch as my mother spoons out three small pieces of broccoli and then practically throws the tuna salad onto my plate.

"Not so much!"

"You need to eat something."

"Just not so much. I hate tuna salad."

"Ok honey. I just want you to eat something."

Everyone sits down, and I slowly cut up the broccoli into the smallest pieces I can make them and eat them, one by one. The smaller I make them the less I can taste them.

"So, Adeline, how is school going?"

"Fine," I reply. My parents are worried and I can tell. This thing has been going on for a while and even though my parents stopped asking me every day how I was, I can tell they still wonder.

"I'm doing ok," I reply. I haven't been myself lately. I guess I'm just under a lot of stress with Payton and all. "I'm sorry. I'm just under a lot of stress right now."

"We know, honey. Just let us know what we can do to help."

"Thanks." I say, pushing away my plate. "I think I'm done."

"OK."

That is all they say. I leave them and go back to my room.

Chapter 7

I am at the dinner table. No one is looking at me. Both my parents are talking but not to me. They are both facing away, eating their dinner. I reach up to grab my fork and eat but I can't move my hand from my side. They both turn to stare at me.

"Can I have some milk?" I ask them.

They both look away and continue on with their conversation as if they didn't hear me.

"May I have some more potatoes?" I ask.

This time they don't even turn towards me. They completely ignore me and continue on with their conversation. I can't even understand what they are saying.

"Mom! Dad! Can I please have something to drink!" I yell. My mouth is so dry it is getting hard to talk.

Suddenly, my mom gets up and takes her plate to the dish washer. She scrapes it off and then returns to the table and takes my dad's plate, doing the same thing. She then returns and grabs my plate.

"I'm not done. May I please have my plate back?" I ask her.

She just continues on her way to the dish washer and scrapes all my food off into the garbage before putting it in the dish washer.

"Mom? Dad?" I ask. They are both leaving and going into the living room. I can hear the TV click on.

I try to move but I can't. I am left alone. Alone.

Chapter 8

When I wake up, the first thing I do is check my video. I flip up the screen to my computer and move the mouse over to the little YouTube symbol.

Underneath the video I posted last night, in small bold letters, is the number 30 million. Thirty million people saw my video!

But who do I have to celebrate with? Nobody knows it's me. I have nobody to share it with. My parents would be worried about me. They wouldn't like me posting about other people.

So, instead of celebrating, I get dressed, pack my bag, grab some breakfast and get in the car.

When I arrive at school, I put my bag away in my locker and then take my seat at the back of the class - same as always.

As the kids start to file in, I can tell there is something different. They are all huddled around in groups, some talking, some watching something. Every once in a while, someone will burst out laughing.

Suddenly, the teacher walks in and everyone stops.

"What's going on?" she asks.

"Someone posted a video of us on YouTube. Whoever they are, they got video of all of us. They even commented. They said Payton was insecure." Randy, who sits in the middle of the popular boys group, says before he bursts out laughing.

Payton turns a bright shade of red. I can feel her glaring straight through me to Randy.

"Well, do any of you know who this is?" asks Mrs. Powes.

"No, her channel is Kendal Cook but there isn't a Kendal Cook in the school. Whoever it is they really got us good. They even did the grade sevens and sixes."

"Ok, Ok. This is pretty exciting but there's no time to discuss this now. Take out your books and continue where we left off.

While I take out my book I can't help but smile. I'm finally being noticed, even if no one knows it's me.

—υνιθυε—

Lunch again. Today I have to get more footage for my video so I can't eat in my room. I quickly grab my food and make my way back to the corner.

I don't notice how fast I'm walking and I don't even notice the foot shoot out from under the table and hit me in the legs. I fall face first. At least my food lands next to me and not on top of me.

"Well, well. That was quite some stunt you pulled, making the video." says Payton, not even bothering to get out of her seat and stand over me.

"I didn't do it." I say weakly. I don't even expect her to believe me.

"Who else would have so much extra time to make that video? They would also have to have no friends and sit alone in that corner because that is really the only possible place for that video to be filmed."

"I didn't do it." I say again.

"Maybe she's right," says Kaitlyn who is sitting beside her. "I mean, she wouldn't have enough brains to do it in the first place and she doesn't even have enough courage to stand up to you, let alone post it on YouTube."

"Maybe you're right. You're a nobody Adeline. I can't believe I actually thought you could do something like that."

She turns around and resumes talking with her cluster of friends.

I'm too tired now to film. I'll just go back to my room and wait it out.

—σπεχιαλ—

When I get home, all want to do is sleep. And that's exactly what I do. I sleep through dinner and don't wake up. Not until morning.

Chapter 9

When I wake up this morning the sun is shining through the windows, lighting up the room. I immediately feel like a weight is lifted off my shoulders. Today is Saturday, so I don't need to go to school.

My favourite thing to do on Saturdays is to bike down to the candy store, get some candy and go to the pond. Just relax.

I lay in bed for a little while, looking out of the windows. It looks so peaceful. A few birds fly across the sky. There are no clouds in the sky.

I finally pull myself out of my daze and get out of bed. I quickly pull on some old jeans and a t-shirt that is too big but has lines of colours shooting off in all directions.

After I get dressed I find my way to the kitchen and quickly jot down a note telling my parents where I am going, even though I go to the same place every Saturday.

Dear Mom and Dad,

I'm biking to the candy store and I might walk around Main Street for a while and then I'm going to the pond. I won't go near the water... promise.

I love you,

Addy

I grab my bike out of the garage and make my way down the twisty turny roads to my first stop; the candy store.

—υνιθυε—

The ride there is long, but there is a nice breeze and that fall smell in the air that makes it seem short and surreal. The sound of leaves crunching under the weight of my tires makes me slip into a dream state.

I have no worries and the world around me seems to crumble away with every sound. The farther I get, the closer I slip into my state.

I know the path so well that when I turn the final corner I automatically get off my bike and lean it against the wall.

I have to shake my head to drag myself back to the real world. Right now, on a Saturday, I don't need to worry.

I grab the golden handle leading into the candy store and pull on it. The door slides open easily.

"Why hello, Adeline. It's good to see you again dear!" Mrs. Clamanci is the shop owner, and she knows me so well because I come here every day Saturday. Once she came to our school to give out free samples of her new fudge. That was a day I actually liked.

"Hello, Mrs. Clamanci!" I reply.

I stroll through the aisles, gazing at shelves upon shelves of different types of candy.

"Did you get anything new?" I ask her. I have already tried every candy she has. I like to be the taste tester.

"Yes, actually. We got a new type of taffy. It's orange mountain stream. I saved you a piece, thinking it would go fast, but no one seemed to like it."

She scurries out from behind her desk and into an aisle not far from me.

I follow where she went, almost bumping into her as she comes back out of the aisle.

"Here it is dear," she says, handing me a package that is wrapped in orange wrapper and has what seems to be a stream running across it.

I open the package and take a bite.

"This is delicious!"

"Well then dear, you can have these too. For the ride home," she says, nodding at my bike.

"Thank you, Mrs. Clamanci."

I find my way back outside, chewing on my taffy. My bike is right where I left it.

I decide to take the main street to the pond. All the people are walking in and out of the shops, some with bags and some with ice cream cones.

Everyone comes to our town to get Mickly's ice cream. They have so many flavours that I don't even have enough fingers and toes to count them. Even double that. But I never get to go in, except for Sundays because every other day Payton works there.

While I watch the othe᷎   e scamper about their lives, I slowly make my way to ᷎   ' have to take a sharp left to get on the right path   ᷎ Street to the paths around the pond.

These paths are covered in red rocks, but you can hardly tell because of all the leaves.

When I finally reach the pond, I drop my bike and walk to the edge of the pond. With every step a bubble of fear rises in my stomach. I almost reach the edge but have to turn around. I sit at least ten feet away from the water. I can't swim at all. Not even if I tried. I would drown in two seconds flat.

A swim in the water isn't what I need to have fun here though. Besides, the water is too cold now anyway.

I'll just take a nap.

I lean back and close my eyes. I fall asleep to the sound of bikes zooming past me on the path above, geese flying in the sky and the subtle sound of waves lapping the shores.

Chapter 10

While I nap I dream about the water. I think about the colour and how something so clean and pure can be so scary. It can take someone's life but yet it gives everyone so much pleasure.

I can hear the sound of the waves through my sleep and it makes me feel happy, like I am one of the waves, innocent and pure. No regrets and no problems. It makes me feel strong, like I am in charge. I can choose to drown someone. To hold them under and not let them come up. Submerge them in myself and keep them as a reminder, slowly fading away at my bottom.

My dream suddenly changes and I am filled with fear. Fear that the water will take me. That one day I will just slip and completely submerge and never resurface. Gasping for air but never receiving any. Never to see the light again.

I am then trapped under the water. I frantically swim trying to get out but it holds me under. I scream and let out all my air. Slowly, I float to the bottom, landing softly on the dirt. I have lost all my energy and I don't want to try to get back up. I let go and let the water take me. I watch it float around me and completely control me. Suddenly, I feel calm, relaxed even. I just let the soft movements of the water rock me back and forth. Small fish swim around me, going about their daily lives. I forget about my life above the water and let the small fish gather all my attention until I have completely forgotten about everything else. Until I just give up and let the fish nibble at my toes, at my fingers. I let the whole world slip away from me. I just don't care and forget about everyone else. I let the strong waves soothe me until I am gone.

Chapter 11

I wake with a start and before I realize where I am I call out, "I slept in!".

Then I realize I just dozed off at the pond.

I find the unopened packet of taffy and chew on it for a while. What time is it? I wonder.

"Um... Excuse me, sir. What time is it?" I ask a man jogging on the path behind me.

"Ah, you are awake. I saw you sleeping there before and thought about waking you but did not. It is 3:00," he says in a very strong French accent before jogging off again.

That means I must have slept for four hours.

I grab my taffy and wrap it back up in the package. I hop back onto my bike and start the ride home.

It doesn't take me long to ride home and, like before, the sound of the leaves crunching under my tires soothes me.

Before I know it, I am pulling into the drive way and up the steps to the front door.

"I'm home!" I yell as I open the front door.

"Hey, Addy. You've been gone a while. Did you have fun?" my dad asks as he comes out of the kitchen, drying a pan.

"Yeah, it was fun. I fell asleep for a little but not for too long."

"That's good. Wash your hands and come to the kitchen for dinner."

"Dinner? What time is it?" I ask him.

"Five fifteen. Your mother has to leave for a meeting so we have to eat earlier."

I must have biked really slow. It seemed like it was three o'clock just a few minutes ago.

I take my seat at the table and let my father spoon the fettuccini alfredo onto my plate.

"That's good," I say. "Thank you."

"So. How was your day? What did you do?" my mother asks as she sits across from me.

"It was good. I got some new taffy from the candy store. Mrs. Clamanci gave it to me." I say, shoving a spoonful of pasta into my mouth after I finish.

"I fell asleep in the park though. That was quite unfortunate." I say, but before I finish, my parents burst out laughing.

"What?" I ask. I can't help but smile.

"Nothing. Nothing," they reply.

"It's just, I have never heard a kid your age say 'it's quite unfortunate,'" my mother says in a mocking tone.

We finish eating and I clear my plate and go back to my room. I was looking at the video I posted again when something hit me. I left my bike by the steps.

I grab my coat and head back outside. Sure enough, my bike was leaning against the steps.

I slowly wheel my bike into the garage and then shut the door behind me. Don't want any burglars.

While I'm walking back into the house I hear voices coming from the kitchen.

"Come on Frank. You know what's going on. She's being bullied. She has been for years. The saddest part is it's killing her. It's changing her. She used to be this beautiful girl who was creative and artistic but now this girl, she's scared all the time."

"Give it some time, Melissa. It will all sort itself out," replies my father.

"You're right. But we have been giving it time. Three years, Frank."

There is a silence and I take this time to quietly shut the door and slip in through the sun room.

—σπεχιαλ—

Every Sunday I have to go to church. We have always gone to church, just me and my mom. My dad doesn't like to go to church because he says he's too busy, but I think he just doesn't like it.

I get up and put on my church clothes - a blue dress that puffs out at the end, kind of like you're standing inside of a bowl. The dress has blue ruffles on it and pink rhinestones along the top edge.

I walk into the kitchen and my mother is standing at the island making breakfast.

"Good morning, sweetheart. How was your sleep?" she asks me.

"Good," I say, grabbing an apple off the counter.

"Ok. We're running a bit late so just take that apple in the car," she says.

I glance over at the clock in the living room and it reads nine thirty.

"Ok," I say. I walk out to the garage and get into the car. A few minutes later my mother walks out and we drive down the road.

We drive in silence to the church which is only a few blocks away.

The church which has a white cross on the top. The whole building is white with brown trim.

I slip out the door and walk over to the entrance of the building.

To be quite honest with you, I don't really like church either. All they do is talk and say prayers. I don't like listening to people sing or pray but I do like to go with my mom. She seems to like it.

We take our seats but my mom walks over to her friends and talks. Videos start to play on the big screen ahead of us and they dim the lights.

I settle down in my seat and prepare for the two hours until church is over.

—υνιθυε—

After they turn on the lights I walk with my mother over to the minister.

We begin the drive home in silence but it doesn't last long.

"So, how was it today?" my mother asks.

"Same old, same old," I reply.

"You know, Addy, you don't have to keep coming with me. It's your weekend. You can do whatever you want."

"I know. But I like coming with you… if it makes you happy."

"It does sweetheart, but you don't need to come all the time."

"Ok. Maybe I'll come every second weekend," I say.

"Sounds good to me."

We finish the drive home and pull into the garage.

"We're home!" I call out as I come into the house.

"How was it?" my dad asks from behind the wall. He must be in the living room.

"Good," I reply.

I walk over to the living room where my father is sitting on the couch.

"What are you watching?" I ask.

"'Naked and Afraid'. Want to watch?" he asks.

"Yeah."

I sit next to him on the couch and spend the rest of my afternoon watching a marathon of 'Naked and Afraid'. A perfect end to a perfect weekend.

I watch the sun go down and prepare myself for what comes tomorrow... another hard day of school. Another hard day of Payton.

Chapter 12

I am running. Fast and far. I can't stop and I can't tell where I am. All I can see are houses. I turn around and I can see my house. Then I feel a backpack on my back.

I want to turn back but I can't stop my feet from moving. I can hear shouting from behind me. I turn around and see my parents running behind me. They are shouting at me to turn around but I can't. I can't stop myself from moving.

"Adeline! Adeline!" They are shouting from behind me.

Then I can hear voices all around me. All of them are calling my name. Finally I stop. I stop and turn around. But my parents are no longer there.

"Adeline." I can hear my mother say from behind me.

I turn around and see a river behind me. My mother is standing in the middle of the river.

"Come Adeline," she says.

"I can't swim." I say.

"Then go. Go away."

I stand there for a minute and then turn to go. I run away again. I run down the street and away. I can feel the hot tears streaming down my face.

My foot catches the curb and I fall to the ground.

Chapter 13

Sunday, Monday. Tuesday, Wednesday. Thursday, Friday, Saturday.

Today is Monday. Monday, Monday, Monday. That is all I can think on the long drive to school. Monday, Monday, Monday.

Today started like any other day but there was something different - something out of place.

Normally when I get to school I am the only one in the parking lot, because I arrive so early, but today I am not alone.

The girl Karlee, from the cafeteria, is sitting in the middle of the field. She looks like she's just sitting there, staring ahead but she must be doing something.

No she's not. She's crazy, remember? How do you know she's not going to flip out at you. Have a panic attack or seizure. She does have Down's Syndrome.

But something draws me over there. I walk carefully, after my mother has driven away.

As I approach her I use the smallest voice I can to squeak out "Hi."

She lifts her head and looks at me through her big blue eyes. Her eyes look like pools and keep me in a trance for a moment and cause me to sit next to her.

"Hello. I'm Karlee," she says after a moment.

"I'm Adeline. What are you doing?" I ask her.

"Counting the flowers," she replies.

I look down and see that, indeed, her hands are wrapped around many flowers.

"Why?" I ask. I wouldn't even think to count the flowers.

"Because I feel like it."

"OK, so how many flowers are there?" I decide to just let it go and move on. I don't know why I'm staying here.

People have started to arrive, and I have missed my opportunity to get in to class early.

Suddenly, Karlee stands up, falling a little which causes me to put out a hand and help her to her feet.

"Thank you." she says, very simply.

I go over the symptoms of Down's Syndrome in my head: small hands, short neck, short fingers. Those are all the physical symptoms I can remember. There is also slow learning, slow speech development and short attention span.

Considering Karlee just sat in this field and counted flowers I don't think that one is a problem for her.

I take another look at her, she does have small hands and has trouble standing up but if you focus on all the things we don't have in common, you will never see what we do.

We both have browny – blond hair. We both have blue eyes, although hers are brighter than mine. But mostly, we are both outcasts.

We continue on together to the school, coming in through the side doors. Karlee slips a little and looks pretty unstable so, as if on instinct, I put my arm through hers.

"I got you," I say in a soothing voice. "What are you doing out here anyway?" I ask as I open the door.

"I don't know," she says simply. "I guess I just wanted to come early. I thought maybe it would be fun,"

"To each his own," I say.

We walk together, into the school, until we have to part ways. Karlee has to go to room 10 with all the other special needs kids and I have to go to advisory.

"Why do you have to go with the other special needs kids, you're pretty smart," I announce.

"We're starting to do immersion classes, where I get to go with the other grade nine classes. But that won't start for a while. Maybe not even this year," she replies.

"That's unfortunate," I don't know what else to say. She is smart and I know she doesn't want to be there, I can tell, even if I just met her.

We finally reach the end of the hall, where the path splits. Room ten is at one end and my class is at the other.

"See you later, Karlee," I say as I let go of her arm.

"Yeah, maybe at lunch. They've been letting me come out to the cafeteria. I guess I'm just not as messed up as they thought I was," she says with a little grin.

"Yeah, maybe," I reply.

I start to make my way back to class, turning back once to see if Karlee was getting there ok. She was making her way to room ten, holding on to the railings they put around the halls for the special aid kids.

"Aw, did you make a new friend. She's a freak like you. Are you really that desperate, you're making friends with the special needs kids?" Payton comes up behind me while I'm watching Karlee make her way down the hall.

I don't feel like fighting, I'm having a pretty good day so far, so I just walk away.

"Hey! I'm talking to you," I can hear her say behind me.

Suddenly I feel a cold hand on my back and I lose my footing and fall over.

"Whatever," she says as she passes me.

—σπεχιαλ—

Lunch finally comes and I make my way over to where I said I would meet Karlee.

When I get there I see Karlee waiting right where I told her to meet me.

"Hello," I say as I walk up to where she is standing.

"Hi."

"How was your morning?" I ask her. She looks bright and perky so I think her day is going ok.

"Ok, how was yours?"

"It was ok," I say. If she's ok, I guess I'll be ok too.

I guide Karlee over to the spot where I sit in the corner.

"This is where I sit most lunches," I say as I take out my camera. "I sit here and film people."

"Cool. Are you allowed to do that?" she asks me.

"Do what?"

"Film the people. What they do, stuff like that."

"I guess. Here, I'll show you."

I pull out my camera and press the big round button. The camera clicks on and starts to record.

I move the camera around the room, getting footage of every person. Payton with her group of mean girls, Rachel and her group, the boys, everyone.

When I finish I shut the camera off and slip it back into my lunch bag.

"No one would expect to find it here," I tell Karlee, answering her unasked question.

When the lunch bell rings I take Karlee to my little room. It takes us a while to get there because Karlee has to steady herself on the railings but we get there just in time to not attract suspicion.

"This is where I go after lunch," I tell Karlee, pointing around the room.

I need to help Karlee across the room to the windows because there aren't any railings in the room.

"I like the view," she says. She speaks with a lisp and the words come out slowly.

We sit there for the rest of lunch talking about the room and about school. She loves school and wishes that people would notice that. We're the same.

I finally have a friend, and it's nice to have someone to talk to.

Chapter 14

"Listen up! Settle down everyone!" Mr. Dunval yells at us from his desk.

We all sit down and look at him, waiting for our next instruction.

"Shakespeare was a great poet," he continues.

"Yeah, and?" asks Ethan.

"Don't push it Mr. Staply," he clears his throat and then continues. "Poetry has taught us all about our past. It inspires us to create great things. For your next assignment, you will be writing your own piece of poetry. Try to make it interesting. If you want a good mark, try to inspire us."

"Isn't poetry just for dead people?" someone from the back of the room calls out.

"No. This project will count for fifteen percent of your mark." That statement is followed by a howl of moans and then the bell rings and the class rushes out the door.

I walk over to meet Karlee by room 10. We walk right over to our room. I don't want to film anything today so we can just relax until the end of lunch.

"We got assigned a poetry project today," I tell Karlee as we walk into the room.

"What are you going to write about?" she asks me.

"I don't know. I'll have to think about it."

"Would you like to come over tonight? If you're not too busy working on your project?"

"Ok. How do we get there?" I ask her.

"I have to go in a wheel chair on the bus and you'll have to push me but it's not too far."

"Ok, I'll just call my mom. I'll be right back."

I walk out of the room and over to where the school phone is. I press nine and dial our phone number.

"Hello," my mother's voice comes from the other end of the line.

"Hi mom, it's Addy. Can I go over to Karlee's house tonight after school until about five thirty?"

"Um… Ok. Will they drive you home?" she asks.

"Yeah I think so."

"Ok. Have fun sweetie."

"Bye Mom."

I hang up the phone and walk back to Karlee.

"So, can you?" she asks me as I walk in.

"Yep."

"Great. Meet me outside room ten at the end of school."

"Got it."

The bell rings and I walk back to class. Only two more periods.

—υνιθυε—

"Hey," I say to Karlee as I approach her. She's standing outside of room ten.

"Hello. Can you get my wheel chair out of the class room?" she asks me.

"Sure," I say. I've never been in room ten before.

I slowly walk into the room and see a black and silver wheel chair sitting against the wall. I grab it and walk back out to where Karlee waits for me.

I lower her down in the chair and begin to push her down the winding halls to the front door.

"Where does your bus pick you up?" I ask her as I open the door leading out of the school. I hold the door open with my body.

"I have to take the handicap bus and it meets me in Conveniently, the parking lot is right outside the doors.

As if on cue, the bus pulls up against the curb and a small ramp shoots out of the open doors in the back.

I push Karlee's wheel chair up the ramp and attach a seat belt across her, keeping her against the wall of the bus.

"Thank you," she says.

"No problem."

The bus ride to Karlee's house is long but Karlee introduces me to all of her friends. Almost all the room ten kids take this bus home. When she's not introducing people to me, she's talking to all of them. Even the ones that can't talk very much which looks more painful for them than it is for her. She just keeps chatting though.

When we finally reach Karlee's stop it's already four thirty so we only have an hour before I have to be home. It takes fifteen minutes to get back to my place and ten for Karlee to get ready so really we only have half an hour to hang out.

"Sorry we don't have that long. I didn't realize how long it took to get home," she says as I push her home.

"That's ok. I never get to see those kids so it was nice to finally meet them."

"Yeah, most of them are pretty nice. Hey! Look at the flowers! I didn't even know they were still growing," she says.

"Yeah, I guess it's not too cold yet," I say.

"Can you go pick some for me?"

"Sure."

I walk over to the flower beds and pick some flowers. When I glance over at Karlee she's looking at me.

I decide to go get her. She'll like it more if she was here anyways.

"Finally! I thought you'd never ask!" she says with a grin as she tries to lift herself out of her chair.

"Easy now," I say.

I walk her over to where I was sitting with the flowers and set her down beside where I was sitting.

"Look at all the pretty flowers," she says.

She picks a flower and holds it up to her nose. Her hand wobbles but she tries to keep it still.

A small ant crawls off the flower and on to her hand, and then another, and then another.

"Karlee, there's an ant on your hand," I say, trying to sound calm for her. An ant isn't a big deal but these are red and I know a symptom of Down's syndrome is a high pain tolerance so they can withstand lots of pain until the pain is so bad that they get seriously hurt, but they don't know they are hurting in the first place.

She looks down at her hand and shakes it off.

"Maybe we should go," she says calmly.

"Yeah."

I look down at my watch, it's five fifteen.

"I guess I have to go as soon as we get back to your place," I say.

"Yeah. That's ok. My mom will drive you."

It only takes us a little while to get to Karlee's house but not enough time for Karlee to drive home with us.

As soon as we get back to Karlee's house I get into her car and her mom drives me home.

It was fun to have a friend, to go to someone's house. I haven't done that in forever.

And it looks like Karlee's mom is thinking the same thing.

Chapter 15

After I got home from Karlee's I went straight to work on my poem for Mr. Dunval.

I take a seat at my desk and pull out a blank sheet of paper. If I can just write out a bunch of ideas for it then I can piece them together. Bitter sweet, twisted lies. I'm trying to make it memorable, trying to base it on something that I can make memorable, from a memory but I can only think about Payton. A poem about bullying won't be too bad either.

Now that I came up with a bunch of ideas for my poem I just have to separate them into ideas. I come up with four different sets of ideas, each consisting of a different meaning or plot.

Now all I need to do is put them all together and come up with a name. I look at the words I have chosen, the theme and stuff, and I decide to call it "People Alike".

—σπεχιαλ—

This morning I was supposed to meet Karlee before school but I had to call and cancel because I wanted to get ready for my presentation in first period.

It feels like old times, walking through the halls before anyone else gets there. Lately I've been walking with Karlee and stay to the side of the halls so she can grab the railings but now I'm alone.

I sit in my corner of the class and go over my presentation. I think it's quite good but most of the time Payton gets the best marks. I wonder what her poem will be about.

All the other kids file in and eventually so does Mr. Dunval.

"Did everyone finish their poems?" he asks us as he walks in, taking his seat at the front of the class.

There is a murmur of agreement around the room.

"Who would like to go first?"

"Me," says Payton.

She walks up to the front of the class and pulls a sheet of paper out of her pocket.

Me, myself and I
I am beautiful, I am strong.
I am better than most because I am my own song.
You can try to be like me,
But it will take hard work and you'll need to fix your teeth.
I am perfect, I am slim,
I am better than you so I will win.

When she finishes, she looks out at the class and accepts the round of applause that follows.

"Now who would like to go?" asks Mr. Dunval.

"I guess I will," says Will.

Like Payton he takes his place at the front of the class and reads his poem.

It goes on and on until I am the only one left to go.

"Adeline, it's your turn," Mr. Dunval says.

I walk up to the front of the classroom. Suddenly I am overcome by a feeling of nervousness, so strong that I have to grab the bottom of my shirt to steady my hands.

I pull the piece of paper out of my pocket and stand at the front of the room.

"Whenever you're ready, Adeline," says Mr. Dunval.

I clear my throat and begin.

People Alike
You may push me down
With your bitter, twisted lies.
You may treat me like dirt,
But like dust I will rise.
You push me away and shade your eyes,
But soon you will see,
You should have looked at me.
You can push me down,
You can hold me down.
But you will see,
I will rise,
And I will fly.

I wait for claps but nothing happens so I go back to take my seat.

"I think that was the best one yet," says Will.

"Great job, Adeline!" says Mr. Dunval. "Give her a round of applause!"

The class claps but the applause is cut short because the bell rings and everyone gets up to leave.

"Nice poem. Did you copy it?" says Payton as she comes up behind me as I'm walking to my locker.

"No," I say, looking straight ahead.

"Whatever," she says and pushes me into the lockers with her shoulder.

I wait for her to turn the corner and then I walk to my locker and put away my stuff. I have to meet Karlee in the supply room but first I have to get my lunch.

I walk carefully to the cafeteria and slip into line. I pick out my sandwich and fruit and then head out of the cafeteria.

"Where are you going?" Payton says.

"Nowhere," I reply.

"Why don't you eat with us? Like a normal person," she says.

I have almost made it out of the cafeteria but Payton has stood up and is following me.

"You know what? Actually you should leave. We don't want you."

I have now made it out of the cafeteria but Payton sticks her leg out and I fall, just outside the doors. She closes the doors to the cafeteria and leaves me outside.

Chapter 16

The rest of the week went by, same old same old. Today, though, I'm taking Karlee to the pond where I go on Saturdays even though today is Friday.

On Fridays, first period doesn't start until nine thirty so we have plenty of time if my mom picks us up at nine.

I quickly get dressed and grab my bike. Karlee said she would meet me at the pond, since her bus ride takes a while so I wouldn't have to get up so early.

I thought about taking her to the candy shop but she needs to be in her wheel chair so it would be hard to get her there.

All the autumn leaves that were there last week have now been covered in a thin layer of snow. It is not too cold to bike yet though. That's the thing about this town, it doesn't get too cold until December but it starts to snow around October. Or maybe we're just used to it.

I finally reach the pond. The snow here has all melted since the sun hits it early. I rest my bike on a tree and sit down next to the water.

A short while later, Karlee's bus shows up and I go over to help her off.

"How are you? Was the bus ride ok?" I ask her as I push her over to where I was sitting.

I haven't gotten to see her much this week, only at lunches.

"Yeah, it was good. How was the bike ride?"

"It's getting pretty snowy to do bike rides."

"Do you want to go near the water? I wonder if it's cold," she asks.

"It's probably really cold if it's started snowing. Besides, I can't swim," I say, looking at my feet.

"Really? Even I can swim. I take swimming lessons on Tuesdays. You can laugh, but I can swim better than I can walk."

"I don't think we should go near the water. It's probably really cold and I can't help you if you get stuck or something. Besides, we have school later," I say looking at my watch. "It's already eight forty. Maybe we should take a walk around the pond."

"Ok."

I help Karlee into her chair and start to push her around the pond.

"I like it here," she says.

"Me too. Even if I can't swim."

The pond isn't very big, so it doesn't take us long to walk around it. Before we know it we're back at the tree and my mom is pulling up.

"Hi mom," I say as I help Karlee into the car and then fold her wheel chair and put it in the back.

"How was the park?" she asks.

We pull out of the park and begin the drive to school.

"You must be Karlee. Hi, I'm Melissa."

"It's nice to meet you," Karlee says.

Karlee and Mom chat the rest of the ride to school but I get distracted and start to look out the window. There are so many people out there that are going about their lives, with their own problems. Sometimes I wish I could stay home and just watch all the people, like I do at school. But, if I want to have a different life, I have to be educated and...

"Addy. Addy."

Someone's shaking my shoulder.

"What?"

"We're here," says Karlee.

"Oh, right."

I get out of the car and unload Karlee's wheel chair.

"Thanks mom."

"You're welcome sweetie. You two have fun at school."

I walk Karlee into the school and to her locker.

"Hey, look!" she says suddenly.

"What?" I ask.

"There are flyers for a school dance! We should go!"

"I don't want to be mean but you're in a wheel chair and I can't dance."

"I can still walk. We can stay along the walls," she says. "Please."

"Ok. But only if I'm here that day."

"Come on. This is your last year here. Try to have some fun."

"Ok. But we'll only go for one hour and we have to stay along the walls."

Karlee looks at me.

"Lighten up. Let go and have some fun."

That really hurt me and she immediately takes it back.

"I'm sorry Addy. I know you have trouble with Payton but don't let that take over your life."

"I never used to be like that. I used to be fun and creative but now I have to hide from Payton. That sounded really cheesy, but it's true."

"I'm sorry, Addy."

"That's ok. Have fun. I'll see you at lunch."

I leave her there and walk back to home room. Maybe she's right. Maybe I should let go. It's about time I go back to the way I was. I can't let Payton take over my life.

Chapter 17

I haven't seen Karlee all day. I decide to sit in the cafeteria and film instead of meeting her in the supply room. I know I probably shouldn't be mad at her and I'm not. I'm just sad because what she said was true. Even my parents think it.

I leave the cafeteria and go to my locker. I have gym next and I have to grab my gym strip.

The bell rings and I hurry off to gym so I can get changed before everyone gets there.

Our gym is small but we have a stage that is attached to the side of it. On the stage we have work out equipment but also wrestling mats since we're doing wrestling in gym right now.

I take a seat on one of the mats on the stage and wait for Mr. MacMillian to come in.

Soon all the girls come on to the stage. We are all dressed in blue t-shirts and black shorts, our school colours. Payton and all those girls wear booty shorts, which are not allowed, but no one seems to notice.

Today is testing day for wrestling so we each have to wrestle one person. Mr. MacMillian pairs us up with someone and we have to wrestle them. If we win we get a perfect mark.

"Ok. Here is the list of people you'll be wrestling. Sophia and Lina. Bella and Brinlyn. Elena and Elisha. Kaitlyn and Kara. Emily and Kendal. Payton and Adeline."

I was expecting that. There are only twelve girls in our class and when ten of them were called, and I wasn't one of them and neither was Payton...

"Sophia and Lina, you will be going first."

I take a seat at the back of the class and wait until it's my turn.

Sophia ends up winning and Lina has to go get ice for her knee.

I don't know why we do this unit if people keep getting hurt but I guess we would need to find another sport to fill up this unit.

"Payton and Adeline, you're up."

I step up onto the mat and stand on one edge of the circle. Payton stands on the other.

"Whenever you're ready, girls."

Payton just stands there so I decide to make the first move. I run at her, trying to hit her legs with my shoulder but she moves out of the way.

She runs at me and I stick my leg out and she falls onto her back on the mat. The crowd cheers.

I leap on top of her, trying to pin her but she rolls over and pins me. I push her off and she stands on her knees. I jump at her and push her over onto her stomach.

She gets up on her hands and knees and I decide to use one of the moves we were taught. I reach for her far arm and her close leg and pull them at the same time, causing her to fall.

She gets back up before I have time to pin her and lunges at me. I fall over and she stands up. Then, out of nowhere, she falls and lands on my wrist. A searing pain runs up my arm and I let out a scream.

"Payton! That was uncalled for! Get away! Everyone clear out!" yells Mr. MacMillian.

He runs towards me and grabs my wrist.

"Does this hurt?" he asks, moving it backward.

"Yeah," I squeak out.

"We've got to get you to urgent care," he says.

He helps me up and I walk out, holding my wrist to steady it.

I wait in a chair at the office while they call my mom and tell her to take me to urgent care.

Soon, she arrives and drives me over to the urgent care which is just two minutes from school.

Since I looked like I was in a fair amount of pain they took me right to the x-ray room.

"How'd you hurt it?" the girl doing my X-ray asks as she puts a grey blanket over top of me and then sets my hand down on top of it.

"We were doing wrestling in gym and a girl fell on me," I say.

She snaps a couple pictures, changing my hand position each time and then lets me leave.

"Wait here," she says leading me to a room with a bed in it. "I'm going to look at the photos and then we can give you a cast or just wrap it."

"Ok, thank you," I say.

"No problem."

With that she leaves the room.

A couple minutes later she comes back.

"I have some bad news. Your hand is broken. We're going to need to put a cast on it."

"Ok, right now?" I ask.

"Yes, follow me."

I follow her into another room that looks like the one I was just in but has a big cabinet on the wall.

I sit down on the bed and she pulls out something that looks like a sock from the cabinet and puts it on my hand. She then wraps the sock in what looks like tensor bandage that is sticky and covered in Paper Mache.

"What colour would you like?" She asks me.

"Do you have purple?"

"Sure thing."

She overlaps the white with a purple bandage.

"Just let it sit for a minute," she says.

She leaves me in the room with my new cast on. It has already started to itch.

She comes back a little later.

"It's all good. Time to go," she says and helps me down.

"Thanks," I say.

I walk back out of the clinic to where my mom is waiting for me.

"Oh, honey! How is it? Do you feel ok?" she asks.

"Yeah, mom. Can we just go home? I'm really tired."

"Ok. Are you sure you don't want to stop for ice cream or something? Do you need to get anything from school?"

"No, I don't feel too good. Can we just go home?"

"Ok. I'll stop and pick you up some ice cream for later anyway."

Chapter 18

I get to school extra early today but not because of Payton, but because it takes me extra long to get to class. My mom comes in with me to help me get my books and carry them to class.

"Thanks mom, but you can go now. Don't you need to get to work?"

"Yes, you're welcome, sweetie."

"Love you mom."

"Love you too."

I give her a hug and then take my seat at my desk. Soon kids start to come in and they all want to know about my wrist.

"What happened?" asks Sophia.

"I broke it wrestling yesterday."

"With Payton?" she asks.

"Yeah."

Soon, I am surrounded by people asking to sign my cast. They all have pens and are scribbling away at it. All I do is sit back and let them write.

When Payton walks in she is greeted by dirty looks.

"How could you do that?" asks Will.

"I didn't," she says.

"Yeah you did," they all say.

"Whatever."

"Guys! She's lying!" pleads Payton.

"Just stop, Payton," says Sophia and they turn their attention back to me.

The bell rings and advisory is over. We all file out of the classroom and make our way to our first period class.

Suddenly, something hits me hard on each side of my shoulder, making me drop my books.

"I can't believe you told them that I hurt you! You will pay for that. They all hate me now!" says Payton.

"Doesn't feel too good does it?" I say.

"What was that? Do you actually have a voice?" she says.

She pushes me into the lockers.

"I don't care if you're hurt. You'll always be a freak."

She walks away but I have to wait for all the people to leave before I get up.

—υνιθυε—

"Hey Karlee!" I say as I approach her.

I told her I would go to the mall with her so she could pick out her dress for the dance.

"Hello."

"Are you ready for the mall?"

"Yeah! I know exactly which dress I want. How's your arm?" she asks.

"Ok. Let's get going though, I have to be home by six thirty."

"Ok."

I push Karlee through the halls and out to where the bus will pick us up. We don't take the school bus this time but we take the city bus since we want to go to the mall.

We get there pretty fast since we don't have to stop and unload at different stops.

We arrive at the mall at four thirty. That gives us one and a half hours to shop before we have to take the bus home.

"I know exactly which store I want to go to get my dress," she says.

"Remember, it might not be there so don't get your hopes up."

"Don't worry. I have five different dresses picked out at five different stores. One of them has got to be here."

I wheel Karlee to her first store, H&M. When we get there she tells me to take her to the dress section.

I help her up onto her feet so she can put her weight on me.

We walk around the dress section looking for Karlee's dress.

"There it is!" she cries out.

I set her down in her chair and go over and look through the dresses.

"What size are you?" I ask her.

"Um… size six."

"Ok."

I look through all the dresses but the only ones that are close are size five and seven.

"How about size five or seven? There isn't a six."

"Ok bring them both and I'll try them on."

I take the dresses and hang them over the back of Karlee's chair. I wheel Karlee over to the change rooms and help her in.

"Are you ok? Do you need my help or anything?" I ask her before I leave.

"No, I should be good."

I close the door and sit down on the benches outside the change rooms.

The dress Karlee picked out was actually quite pretty. It was pink with a white bow on the front.

"Ok. I'm done," says Karlee from the change room.

"How'd it go?" I say as I open the door.

"Not good. The dresses were too small or too big. I guess I can only have a size six. Doesn't matter though, store number two!"

"Ok."

I bring her chair and we make our way to our next stop, Aeropostale. The store is having a sale right now, and that is a bonus.

"Ok, which one is it this time?" I ask Karlee as I wheel her over to the dress section.

"I don't know, I don't see it."

I leave her chair in the centre and walk over to where the dresses are. There are only a few dresses so I can hold them up and ask Karlee if any of them are the ones she wants.

"No. No. No," she says. "I don't think it's here."

"Ok. Where to next then?"

"Le Chateau."

"Let's go."

I wheel Karlee down to Le Chateau. As we pass we can see some of the dresses in the window.

"That's the one!" yells Karlee.

"Ok, Ok! Calm down! No need to yell!"

I wheel Karlee into the store and we go to the display with all the dresses from the window.

"Look Karlee, size six!" I tell Karlee as I grab the dress off the rack.

"Yay. I don't even have to try it on, we already know it will fit."

"Are you sure?" I ask.

"Yeah, besides, the bus is coming soon. It's already ten to six."

"Ok."

I wheel Karlee outside just in time to catch the bus home.

"Thanks for coming with me, Addy. I had a lot of fun," says Karlee as we got on the bus.

"You're welcome. It was fun."

Chapter 19

Today started out like any other day but today I am going back to the mall to pick out the fabric for my dress.

I don't really like normal dresses. They are too frilly and I have a very different style from normal people. I like colours and I like different stuff, being different. But I don't like it too girly. That's why I have to make my own.

So off to the mall again...

On the drive over all I can think of is my dress. It must be a little easier to find fabric than an actual dress. It felt like we were there forever looking for Karlee's dress but frankly I just don't have the time. I have to find the fabric and then make my dress all before Wednesday.

We pull up slowly into the big parking lot of Fabric Land. The Fabric Land in our town is huge compared to the number of people that I know that sew.

"Hey, honey. I think I'm going to go to Safeway but I'll be back in half an hour to pick you up. Is that OK?"

"Yeah, that's good. I'll meet you outside the doors?"

"Ok," she says and drives away.

I make my way to the big sliding doors. Swiftly, I walk through the big doors which part as I approach them. When I first get a glimpse of the store, the aisles are stacked with shelves and shelves of different types of fabric. There's fabric hanging from racks and hangers surrounding the store. In some sections there are mannequins that are dressed in outfits made with the fabric displayed on a rack behind the mannequin.

I decide to look at the fabric hanging on racks first because it's easier to look at than trying to sort through a pile. I decide to get a basket and just take anything that I like and then I'll sort through it later.

I browse through the different racks and shelves gazing at the multi-colored fabric on the shelves. There are

only about three other people in the store and all are probably in their late fifties. So in other words, I am the only one without wrinkles.

As I look through different piles, I spy a particular fabric peeking out from the side of a pile. I give it a small tug and it breaks loose.

The fabric starts off neon pink and then about a third of the way down it changes to bright yellow and then changes to neon blue for the rest of the way down – it's the perfect fabric for my dress. It's hard to look at but that is just the way I like it. I add it to the basket and then continue to look.

I cruise along the racks looking at all the fabrics. One of the mannequins is wearing a lavender coloured dress that puffs out at the end just the way I wanted my dress to look. It looks like she shoved herself in a cup but put on a tank top before she dove in.

I find my way down to the accessories aisle where they have the beads and gems. I really want some sparkles to brighten up my dress.

For one small aisle, they have a lot of sparkles. The whole row is filled with different coloured sparkles. Not only sparkles but also jewels and little fabric flowers and bows.

I pick out every colour possible of sparkles and four packages of rhinestones - orange, green, pink and purple. I also pick out two packets of flowers, one blue and one purple.

I just have to sort through all my stuff now. I have so much my cart is overflowing. I walk over to a small bench on the other end of the aisle. As I unload my cart I sort out all the things I don't want and all the things I want to keep.

After some consideration, I decide to take out all the fabrics from the pile except for the multi-coloured one. I also keep the orange and green gems and the purple flowers - plenty for my dress.

The lines aren't too long and I get out in five minutes, just in time for my mom to pick me up.

"How'd it go sweetie?" she asks as I get in the car.

"Good! I got some really cool fabric and some cool things to go on it," I say.

"That's fantastic! Do you need any help sewing?"

"No, I think I've got it."

Chapter 20

Today is the day of the dance. I still need to finish my dress and buy the tickets for me and Karlee. Karlee can't do it because she has to stay in room ten for a presentation all day.

I hope they set up a booth at the front office again this year because then I can stay in at lunch and I won't have to come out.

Luckily they do, but I don't get there nearly early enough. There is a line coming from the booth that looks like at least a twenty minute wait. And Payton just happens to be one of the people in line.

I slip into line behind the last person and wait patiently for my turn. The principal has made an announcement that students will be late for first period because the lines are so long.

Finally it is my turn to get tickets.

"How many would you like?" the girl at the front asks me.

"Two please," I say.

I hand her eight dollars, four each, and she gives me my tickets.

I try to leave there as fast as I can and get back to class but Payton steps in my path. It's like she is just stalking me and lays awake at night planning different ways to bully me.

"Why do you think you can go to the dance?" she says.

"Because I bought tickets," I say.

"You don't even have anybody to go with. You will ruin the mood by sitting in the corner alone," she spits.

"Actually I'm going with Karlee," I say.

"Oh two freaks together. I'm surprised she can even stand up."

And then, in one well-practiced move, she takes my tickets and rips them in two, throwing the pieces at me.

"Freak," she says and then walks away.

I turn back to the end of the line and wait for my turn again.

"Here," someone says from behind me.

I turn to see the girl that gave me my tickets standing behind me, holding out two more tickets.

"I saw the whole thing," she says.

"Thanks," I say, taking the tickets.

It's going to be a long day, I think to myself as I walk back to class.

—σπεχιαλ—

As soon as I get home I work on my dress.

I have already cut out the shape of the dress so now I just have to fold it over and sew the seam shut.

I plug in the sewing machine and slowly feed the fabric through the machine and it spits it out the other side, sewn together.

I sit there for five minutes, just feeding the fabric through. Finally it comes to the end and I am left with the top of my dress. Now all I have to do is attach the circle that I cut out yesterday to the dress.

After more feeding and more sewing the parts are all attached to the end of the dress. Now all that is left are the flowers and rhinestones.

I take out all the rhinestones and attach them in a curvy pattern on the left side of the dress, going all the way down to the bottom of the skirt. The rhinestones are easy because they are the kind that comes with super glue on the back, which I obviously get stuck all over my room. The green and orange rhinestones really look cool with the pink, blue and yellow fabric.

Next I attach the purple flowers. These I have to sew on. No matter, it only takes me about three minutes to attach all the flowers and my dress is finished. I sew on one on the top left corner, one on the middle right and the last one on the bottom left.

Now that my dress is finished I still have some time before I have to go to Karlee's house so I pull out my computer from one of my desk drawers and open MG Movies. I can add some background music and do some finishing touches to my video, which I have now made into a full-length movie about my life. I titled it "The Inside Scoop on a School Girl".

Suddenly, my phone rings. I reach over and take it off its charger.

"Hello," I say upon answering.

"Hi, it's Karlee," she says.

"Oh, hey," I say.

"Hey. Are you ready for tonight?" she asks me.

"Yeah I guess. How are you going to dance with your chair?" I ask.

"Um... I don't actually need my chair. I just like to use it because then people won't push me around. I'm afraid they'll make fun of me but if I'm in a chair then they kind of back off. Does that make sense?" she asks me, kind of laughing.

I think about it for a minute. It's kind of like why I hide in our room at lunch. I just never thought Karlee was afraid of anything.

"Yeah, it makes a bit of sense. So are you going to bring it tonight?" I ask, moving to sit on my bed.

"That's why I called. I don't think I want to. But I'll need you to look out for me."

"Of course. Do you still want me to come at six?"

"Yeah. See you then," she says.

"Yeah, bye," I say and then hang up.

I glance over at the clock and it's already five thirty.

Better put my dress on, I say to myself.

I change my tank top to a pink one and slip on my dress over top. The dress poofs out at the waist, exactly the way I want it to. It makes me look like I'm wearing a colourful cupcake but I love it.

I skip out into the living room and stand in front of the TV where my parents are both watching "Naked and Afraid".

"Look," I say.

"Wow, Addy! You did a great job!" my mom says.

"Addy it's beautiful!" agrees my dad.

"Thanks," I say.

There is still twenty minutes until I have to go to Karlee's so I take a seat in the chair and watch the end of the show.

Chapter 21

Ding Dong. I ring the doorbell at to Karlee's house.

"Hi," she says as she pulls open the door.

"Hi."

I notice she isn't using her wheel chair.

"You know, you really are a good actor. You got me believing that you needed that chair but look at you! You can walk just fine!" I say as I walk in and take my jacket off.

"Yeah, maybe I should be an actor," she says.

"Wow," she says as she turns around. "I love your dress!"

"Thanks," I say. "I made it myself."

I pull out a hanger from the small closet beside the door and hang my coat up.

"Do you want anything to eat?" Karlee calls from the kitchen.

"No thanks," I say. "You know they serve food at the dance."

"Oh, right!" she calls.

I follow her voice into the kitchen.

Karlee has a small house that's only one floor. The kitchen is open just like ours and goes right into the living room. Across from that is a long hallway with three doors coming from it. I'm guessing it must be the bedrooms and a bathroom.

I turn back to Karlee who is pouring herself a glass of juice.

"We should probably get going," she says between gulps from her glass.

I glance over at the clock and it reads six fifteen.

"Yeah, you're right. If we want to get there at six thirty we should probably go."

Karlee walks back over to the closet and takes out a coat for her and my coat.

"Here you go," she says as she hands it to me.

"Thank you, thank you very much." I say, trying my best to sound like Elvis.

"You trying to sound like Mr. Presley there?" she asks as she puts on her coat.

"Yeah."

"Mom! We're ready to go!"

"Ok, Love! Get in the car! I'll be there in a sec!" she calls from her bedroom.

I push open her front door again and we get into her small car.

"Are you excited?" Karlee asks me as I buckle up my seatbelt.

"Yeah, are you?" I ask.

"Yes! I can't wait!" she replies.

"Are you girls ready?" Karlee's mom asks as she gets in the car.

"Yeah!" we both exclaim.

The whole ride there we just talk about the dance. What it will look like, what food they will have, what music they will play.

Finally we get to the school and it has already gotten dark.

"All of you out! Here we are!" she says.

"Thanks Mom," Karlee says as we get out of the car.

"Have fun you two!" she calls at us.

"See you later!" Karlee calls back.

Karlee and I walk into the dance together. The music is pounding from the gym doors as we walk in. The gym is decorated with stars and the Eiffel Tower. The theme of the dance must be Paris. I can hear #Selfie playing in the gym and everyone is already dancing.

"Let's go!" screams Karlee as she runs into the dance. I follow behind her into the array of green and yellow lights.

Karlee stops at a spot behind the crowd that has formed in front of the speakers and starts to dance. I join her and we dance to the last part of #Selfie and the first part of Roar.

"Look! A photo booth! We should go!" Karlee screams over the music.

"Ok!" I say.

We weave through the crowd towards the photo booth at the other end of the gym. We both pile in and take a seat on the bench inside the machine. Everybody is too busy dancing to be in the photo booth.

"Ok, let's do goofy." Karlee says.

We booth stick out our tongues and wait for the flash of the camera.

"Ok now sophisticated," I say.

We pose with our legs and hands crossed.

"Ok, how about fishy faces?" she says.

We both pose with our lips out and I hold my hand up in a peace sign.

"Ok, I think that's it," she says.

I hop out first and Karlee follows. She punches in two to a keypad and the machine prints out two copies.

"Let's go back and dance!" I say.

The DJ starts to play "Slide to the left," a song that we have to dance to in gym class. Everybody gets in lines and we all dance along to the instructions that the song gives us.

When the song finishes, Karlee and I go to the back of the gym to rest for a bit. Suddenly, Payton comes over to us.

"Well, well, well. Looks like you got more tickets then," she says. "Look at your dress, it looks like a rainbow threw up on you!"

"Payton just go away! Leave us alone!" says Karlee.

"Look at Ms. Feisty over there," says Payton calmly.

"Maybe I need to teach you a lesson!" she yells and throws her glass of punch on me and Karlee.

"See you tomorrow Adeline and Friend," she says as she walks away.

"My dress!" I scream.

"It's ok, it will wash out," Karlee reassures me.

"Let's just go home," I say. I'm soaking wet and tired. I just want to go.

"Ok," she says.

We walk out of the gym and away from the loud music. Why does Payton have to ruin everything?

"I'm sorry Karlee, I know how much you wanted to go to this but I'm all wet," I say.

"That's ok, it wasn't going to be any fun if we were all wet. And besides, she probably would have just done something else to us if we stayed. It was fun while it lasted though."

We walk back outside where Karlee's mom is going to pick us up.

"I should probably call my mom, she doesn't know that we want to be picked up early," says Karlee and she walks back into the school to call her mom.

I sit outside by myself. It is getting colder at night now and I'm getting chilled. I wrap myself in my jacket and wait for Karlee to return.

"She'll be here soon, she is just at the gas station so maybe three minutes," Karlee says as she runs to sit beside me.

"That was actually pretty fun, while it lasted," I say.

"Yeah, it was fun to just go and see. I'm not much of a dancer anyway," she says jokingly but I can tell she is really upset that we couldn't stay. I wanted to stay too but not like that, not with everyone staring at us.

Eventually Karlee's mom pulls up and we both get in.

"I'm sorry to hear that you girls had to leave early," she says as we get in. "And you were so excited. That's a shame."

"Yeah," I reply.

"That's ok though. There will probably be other dances. Maybe next year."

"Yeah, there will probably be more dances," Karlee says.

It doesn't take long for us to get to my house. By now I'm really tired even though it is only around eight.

"Thanks for the ride, Mrs. Jansen," I say as I get out.

"No problem," she replies.

"See you tomorrow, Karlee," I say.

"Yeah, bye Adeline," she says.

I get out and walk inside.

"How was it? You're back early," my parents say from the living room.

"It was ok. I'm really tired though."

"Ok, sweetie. Just go right to bed. Are you feeling ok?" my mom asks.

"Yeah, just tired."

"Ok, night Addy," they say.

"Night."

I take off my dress and slip into my pyjamas as soon as I get into my room. Without even brushing my teeth I slide into bed and fall asleep as soon as my head hits the pillow, without even turning off the light.

Chapter 22

"Did you see Adeline last night? She was a mess!"

I can hear all the people talking about me. The praise for my dress was short lived and now, like they completely forgot, all they can talk about is the show-down with Payton. Which, of course, I lost.

"Well, Well, Well. Have fun walking home wet last night?" asks Payton.

Of course she's here. She's always here.

Just keep walking, I tell myself.

"Um... I'm talking to you," she says again.

Just keep walking.

"Don't you know your manners?" she says.

I can hear her speed up and eventually she is right beside me.

The oh-too-familiar pain in my leg comes but this time Elisha pushes me up against the lockers.

"She was talking you," she says as she leans into my ear.

Payton takes Elisha's spot and leans in real close and says, "You are nothing. One day, you will be gone and the world will go on living. Like you were never here and no one will remember you."

She lets me go and walks away.

I slide down the lockers and sit on the ground.

Bring, Bring, Bring. The bell goes. I might as well just go straight to gym. I'm already late for advisory.

I head over to my locker and quickly take out the small, Lululemon bag containing my gym shorts, shirt and shoes.

Gym would probably have to be my worst subject. For one, I almost always have to go alone when we need partners so then I can't do the drill properly. Secondly, I am not a very good at sports. I like running and biking but I don't really work well with other people. Well, other people that I know.

When I reach the gym, I walk across to the change rooms. Inside of our change room is a small bathroom, and then a long bench that goes along the wall. On the side opposite the bench there are five showers, but nobody actually uses them, sometimes they get changed in them though.

After I pull on my top and shorts I return to the gym and take my seat in our "squads." Mr. McMillian sits on a bench facing the wall.

"Good morning," he says without lifting his head from the computer.

"Good morning," I say back.

"Are you ready for some dancing," he asks me.

"No."

"Well, the good news is there are too many girls for boys so some of you get to dance together."

He obviously didn't see who I was because why would I want to dance with other girls?

Before I can answer, some boys come out of the change room and take their seats in the squad and Mr. McMillian's attention is drawn from me to them.

When everybody emerges from the change rooms, Mr. McMillian blows his whistle and yells out 'shin tag'. Everybody immediately gets up and runs around the gym trying to avoid other people, but slapping their legs at the same time.

I run around with all the other kids but most of the time I just end up running laps. I try to hit other people, but no one returns my efforts, so it makes me look like the weird girl trying to play with the big kids.

"Ok, ok!" shouts Mr. McMillian.

Everyone comes back and takes their seat in their squads again.

"So, today we will be starting our dance unit. Now, as you might see we've got a little thing called 'there's too many girls for boys' going on here. So, some girls will be paired up with each other. I will now read out the list of partners.

Of course I get paired up with Payton. At least this time it's not wrestling.

"Ok, we're going to start with something a little easier. Remember the butterfly?" he asks.

A chorus of murmurs emerges from the crowd.

"Ok, get with your partner and we'll start."

Everyone gets up and spreads out around the white lines of the gym. I look around the gym and see Payton standing by herself. I carefully approach her and stand beside her.

"Ready?" he asks us.

Without waiting for an answer he starts the music. I turn to face Payton and hold up one of my hands.

"This is so stupid," she says before she puts her hand in mine.

The way the dance works is basically a slow dance. Right, left, right. Left, right, left. Occasionally Mr. McMillian will call out turn and we have to turn our partners.

Since we got started late we only had time for a couple of songs. Our classes are really short here so we only ever have enough time for one or two things.

Before our second song starts, an announcement comes across the speakers.

"Adeline Jamieson to the office please, Adeline Jamieson to the office, thank you."

I glance over at Mr. McMillian and he gives a slight nod so I know I'm allowed to go. I leave Payton and run over to the office, through the two blue doors that separate the gym from the hall.

As I approach the secretary's desk, the nice one (the one that sits closest to the hall), greets me.

"Hi Adeline! Your mom is here to sign you out. She's waiting for you outside so just go on ahead and get changed and then you can leave," she says.

"Thank you," I say as I turn back to the gym and scurry off.

"You got to go then, I take it." Mr. McMillian asks as I re-enter the gym.

"Yeah," I reply.

"Well, have fun."

It takes me ten seconds flat to get changed and then I rush off to my locker to collect my bag and head out the doors. Our grey truck is parked along the curb.

"Hi," I say as I hop in the front seat.

"Hello," she replies.

"Where are we going?" I ask.

"To get an X-Ray for your arm."

"Oh."

"So how was school?" she asks me.

"It was ok. I've only had gym though. Why did I even have to come today if I just have to leave now?"

"Because. You miss a lot of school, Addy."

"I do not." I reply. "I miss a sufficient amount of school."

"I've never heard you say that before. I'm glad that school's at least teaching you some great descriptive words! For all the trouble it causes you."

"Yeah." That's all I can say.

The rest of the time I sit in silence, listening to "Summer Time Sadness" on the radio. I hope my hand is healed but for now I just focus on the lyrics of the song running through my head.

I barely notice that we have pulled into the driveway of the clinic and my mom is getting out.

"Coming sweetie?"

"Oh, yeah."

I get out of the car and walk into the clinic. Normally it's quite busy but today, oddly enough, we are the only ones in the waiting room.

I take a seat in one of the big, comfy chairs while my mom goes up and checks us in.

"Ok sweetie. She said that you can go back right now and take a seat in the X-Ray room."

"Already?" I ask. It normally takes forever for us to get through so I'm surprised it is so quick today.

"Yeah. Would you like me to come with you or do you think you can handle it?"

"I think I can handle it," I say. I've been in here a lot lately so I think I can do it.

"Ok, see you soon. I'll just be out here."

"Ok." I say. I lean over and give her a quick kiss. "Love you."

"Love you too, sweetie."

With that, I get up and leave. I have walked these halls before and memorized the very number of rooms there are. In a matter of minutes, I have passed the blue-green curtains of the bedroom part of urgent care and have entered the small waiting room of the X-Ray wing.

As I approach the desk, the lady perched behind it looks up and greets me with a big smile.

"Adeline! Back again? How's it feeling?" she asks me. Her big blue eyes shine up at me and for once I think one person actually cares when they ask me. Most people are just trying to make conversation when they say that.

"It's feeling ok. It doesn't hurt anymore. And I think I'm getting the hang of it, carrying my stuff and stuff like that I mean."

"That's good. It's not too busy today so I think you can come right in. The doctor's free, he might just be a minute," she says.

"Ok."

I walk into the x-Ray room that I have been to many times before. The room always smells like stress though. The people working there late wanting to get home, people wanting to have something broken so they can tell their friends the story, and people dreading having something broken and hoping they can hit the slopes again.

In one corner of the room there is a large machine that processes the X-Ray. In the centre there is a small bed that has an even bigger machine that could very well frighten a small child, hanging over top of it.

I take my seat on the bed and wait patiently for the doctor to arrive. Minutes later, Dr. Pagkoph enters.

"How's it going, Adeline?" he asks.

"Ok, I guess," I say, smiling and lifting up my arm.

"That's good. Now, you haven't been wearing this thing too long, have you?" he asks me. He never takes his eyes off his clipboard, as if to record our conversation.

"No I haven't, about a few weeks. But I have come in a few times because it was rubbing and hurting my arm."

"Ok, so we won't be seeing any major improvements. Have they given you a new cast yet?" still staring at his clipboard.

"No."

"Ok, so that is what we'll do today. Just lay down there and we'll get a quick X-Ray and then I can change your cast."

"Ok."

I lie down on the bed and wait as Dr. Pagkoph pulls out the brown mat to cover the rest of my body from the harmful rays coming from the machine. Next, he pulls down the large machine and places it over my hand and wrist.

"Stay just... Like... that," he says, concentrating so hard he can't even keep his words in one smooth sentence.

He walks back to the desk where the computers that read the X-Ray are and then presses a few buttons on the machine. When he's finished, the machine makes a loud sound, like an oversized camera.

"Ok, just one more," he says as he walks over to me. He turns my arm, so it's on its side instead of flat. He swiftly walks back to the machine and presses the buttons.

"Ok. You should be done. If you want to come back here, we can look at the X-Rays," he says as he helps me down.

I follow him back to the room where he was, and he brings up a picture onto the screen.

"See, there is your wrist and you can still very clearly see the break."

The picture is completely black but my hand is white. There is a very small but visible crack in my bone and it doesn't look like there's any improvement.

"I think you will still have to wear your cast for at least four more weeks," he says as he writes his sentence down on his clipboard. "Do you want your mom to come in and see or do you think you can tell her?"

"I'll just tell her. It doesn't look like anything's improved from the last time anyway."

"Ok, come back in two weeks and we'll see again," he says.

"Ok, thank you."

"You're welcome," he says and hurries out the door to his next patient.

I walk back through the halls to the waiting room of the urgent care wing. I knew nothing would change but for some reason this disappoints me.

"How'd it go?" my mom asks as I enter the waiting room. She gets up and walks toward the door, still looking at me but obviously eager to leave.

"Fine, we have to come back in two weeks. Nothing much has changed," I say.

"Oh, that's ok. It's only been a few weeks anyway."

"Yeah, let's just go home."

"Ok."

We walk out of the clinic and into the parking lot where our car is parked.

"Sweetie, would you be interested in maybe switching schools?" she asks me as we get into our car.

"Why? What about Karlee? Where would she go?" I ask her.

"It's not about Karlee right now. I'm asking you. What do you want to do?"

"I want to stay with Karlee. I can't just leave and let Payton win. Besides, it's getting better now," I say. I just want to make her feel better.

"Ok. Whatever you say. Your father and I just want you to be happy."

"I am. It's getting better, I promise." A little white lie won't kill anyone. Besides, it is getting better, in baby steps.

Chapter 23

Everyone is dancing circles around me. I am standing in the middle and they are all partners around me. Even Karlee. They all have partners and they are all staring at me.

Suddenly, music starts and they all start moving. I stand, glued to the floor, in the centre. Every time someone passes me they whisper something in my ear. All of them are laughing and talking with each other but as soon as they get close to me they stop and just glare.

"Freak," Payton says as she passes me.

Every time someone whispers something it cuts just a little deeper, until I crumble to the ground in a ball.

The voices get louder now, as if they want me to hear them, banging against my ears. Everyone picks up dancing, faster and faster until everyone is blurry. I close my eyes tight and wait until I wake up, willing myself to wake up, but I can't. The music slows and one last person approaches me. Karlee.

"Just disappear," she says.

Her words cut like a sword and leave me lifeless. I never thought I would hear Karlee say that to me. It hurts me and for a split second I believe her. Maybe it would just be better if I disappeared. But then I remember it is just a dream - one of the dreams that haunt me in the night, shouting cruel and scary ideas at me.

Chapter 24

I'm really starting to hate having this cast on. It's so hard to do things. I can't type. I can barely carry my books. Good thing Karlee isn't using her wheel chair anymore because if she was, I wouldn't be able to push her.

At least tomorrow is Friday, and that is good for a few reasons.

I can go to the pond and candy store the following day, like always.

No more Payton for the weekend.

And Fridays are short days. We only need to go to school until one thirty.

But there is still one more day. For me, Thursdays are always the hardest. But I've got to hang in there. I roll myself out of bed and hobble into the kitchen.

"You look exhausted," my dad says.

"Yeah."

I don't really feel like talking. All I want to do is sleep. I can't even find a way to wake myself up. I try to splash water on my face but nothing works. Finally, I just give up and succumb to the sleepiness.

"Adeline... Wakey wakey." I can hear my dad's voice floating in and shattering the barrier of glass that makes all outside world sounds faint and muffled.

"What?" I say as if I'm finally hearing. The glass barrier shatters.

"You've got to get ready for school. It's already eight o'clock."

I quickly glance over at the clock on the microwave. It reads eight o'clock. I must have fallen asleep on the couch. I jump up causing all the blankets to fall to the ground and rush into my room to brush my teeth and get dressed.

I don't even have enough time to brush my hair, which is just one of those thoughts I push to the back of my mind. As if on cue, my mom appears from her room, all dressed and neat.

"Addy, are you ready?" she asks.

"Yes Mom. I've just got to find my bag."

I grab my bag and toss it onto the counter and start shovelling books into it. Then I realize I can't find my math book.

"Mom! Have you seen my math book?" I shout to her from the kitchen.

"No, where did you last have it?" she says from the bathroom.

"On the counter."

"Well look for it. You can't leave without it."

I scramble around the house looking under stacks of books for anywhere that my blue math textbook could be hidden. But it's nowhere.

Now, our house looks like a tornado went through it. Books are on the floor, drawers are open. Then something catches my eye - a corner of a little blue book hiding under a pillow on the couch. I quickly grab it and shove it into my bag, as if it will run away.

"We can go now! I found it!" I shout to my mom while quickly glancing at the clock. Eight twenty five.

I get to school right on time today because of my little math textbook incident. Well, late by my standards.

So I get to spend fifteen minutes weaving my way through the crowd and trying to see through the mob of legs and arms that crowd my face. It's a lot harder to find your way to your locker when the whole school and half the school's parents are trying to do the same thing.

Finally, I reach my locker. It's much quieter in the grade nine wing because hopefully, by grade nine, you will have stopped needing your parents to actually come in the school.

I told Karlee I would meet her at her locker and then give her the plans for tonight (we are going to the candy store). I grab my books and walk to class. I set my books down and make my way to Karlee's locker.

Most of the crowd has cleared out of the hall in front of the special needs rooms so I get there in record time. I get a glimpse off Karlee's bright sweater, but she is backed up against a wall. Karlee doesn't need to go near the walls anymore since she told everyone that she doesn't need her wheel chair.

Suddenly, I realize that Karlee is talking to someone. Who though? I creep a little closer to hear the conversation that's going on.

"-Say that you don't actually need the wheel chair. Why would you do that?" I recognize that voice. Payton.

"No. No I..."

"No. No," she says mockingly. "You deserve Adeline. You're both stupid and you both are alone."

Payton kicks Karlee in the shin and pushes her against the wall. Karlee cries out in pain and grabs her shin.

"Oh, baby," she says.

I can't stand to watch Karlee get hurt. I push through the crowd and, in one big stride, step in front of her.

"Payton! Stop! What did she do to you? You know why she was using that wheel chair? She didn't want to get hurt! She knew this would happen to her so she did this to avoid it."

"Did she now? You know, I don't really care. And there is nothing you can do about it. You are too small to ever stand up to me. Who would back you up anyway? Her? You needed to stand up for her!" And with that, she stalks off.

Chapter 25

"Are you ok?" I ask Karlee, as I turn around to her.

"Yeah, I'm ok," she says rubbing her shin.

"Follow me," I say and turn around.

I twist through the halls and find my way right out through the door.

"Where are you going? Adeline!" she says as she grabs my arm and yanks me back.

"Let's go somewhere. Away. Maybe the candy store?" I ask. I just want to get Karlee away from her. I don't want what happened to me to happen to her. She stares at me for a long time and then agrees.

"Luckily for us, I think I have a toonie in my pocket," I say.

In almost no time we make it down to Main Street. I like to take a shortcut through the park and down the hill. That takes us alongside the highway but luckily there is a crosswalk just a few feet from the path. From there, we run across and past the gas station, past the train tracks, and we make it to Main Street. When I timed it, it only took us six minutes.

Karlee pushes open the small door of the candy store and holds it open for me as I walk inside. I am greeted by the sweet smell of fudge and chocolate. I walk straight over to the large bins that hold the smaller candies.

"Hello Adeline! What are you doing here?" asks Mrs. Clamanci as she walks out of the back room.

"Um... I had a spare," I say. I have never lied to her before but I am doing this for Karlee.

"Oh, ok. Can I get you girls some fudge? On the house!" she asks.

I can't lie to her and take her fudge so I turn down the offer.

"Ok," she says, and she continues to work behind the counter.

"Put your stuff in the bag," I say to Karlee.

I walk around the counters, picking out small candy with the tweezers and keeping track of how much it costs.

"I get one dollar and you get one dollar," I say.

"Ok."

I pick out all my favourite candy, the gummy worms, the sour keys, the berries. Once I pick out all my candies and place them in the bag, I carefully calculate the cost.

"Are you done?" I ask Karlee from across the table.

"Yeah, I think I got it."

We walk over to the counter where Mrs. Clamanci is waiting patiently for us.

"That'll be one ninety-eight," she says.

I hand her over the toonie and she gives me two pennies.

"See you soon, girls," she says as we leave.

"Bye," we both say.

"Where to next?" Karlee asks me as we exit the store.

"The pond of course!" I say jokingly.

I start to run ahead.

"Where are you going? Wait for me!" Karlee yells from behind me.

I never would have thought I'd be running with Karlee. Just a couple of days ago I thought she needed a wheel chair. But for once, I feel happy.

In minutes we have reached the pond. I lean against a tree and give Karlee time to catch up.

"I've got to go running more!" she says and collapses underneath the tree.

"Yeah, how are you supposed to make track?" I ask, smiling. She punches me in the arm and I slide down to sit next to her.

"I would suggest a walk but I think we are both too tired for that," I say.

"Why don't we just sit here and eat our candy. Relax for a little."

I pull the candy bag out from my pocket and place it between us.

"There," I say.

I look around the pond as we munch on our candy.

"It's so nice here. Look at all the birds!" I say.

"Yeah, I really love birds. I always wished I could fly," says Karlee.

I find this a weird thing for a girl who, until recently, I thought needed a wheel chair.

"I'm actually really tired," says Karlee out of nowhere.

"Ok, you've had a big day. Just relax. I'll wake you when we have to leave."

"Ok," she says, without a fight.

She lays down and closes her eyes. Within minutes, I join her.

—υνιθυε—

"Karlee! Karlee Wake up! It's three! We gotta head home!" I yell. Karlee and I must have fallen asleep and lost track of time.

"What?" she says as she gets up.

"We have to go home now or they'll know we skipped! Do you know the way to your house? I don't have time to walk with you."

"Yeah I can get home," she says. "Thanks for helping me today. I really needed it."

"No problem. You would have done the same for me," I say.

I give her a hand up and she stands and brushes the grass off her legs.

"See you tomorrow," she says.

"Yeah."

She leaves and I start the walk home. I end up running because I am short on time and get home pretty fast.

"I'm home!" I yell as I walk through the door.

"Hey Addy!" my parents call from the kitchen.

"I'm going to my room!" I call back as I head to my room.

I shut the door and pull out my computer from under the desk. I really want to finish my movie before next weekend. I'm practically done. I have enough footage but for some reason it's taking me forever to put it all together. I just can't find the right music and backgrounds. I want it to be perfect.

Chapter 26

I have this feeling that somehow my parents found out about yesterday but I don't really care. I don't know if that's just me giving up on myself or if I am starting to regain hold of my life.

School again today but today is Friday. Lovely, lovely Friday. If I have to state the reasons I love Friday again, here they are:

No Payton for two whole days.

Short days on Friday; only until one thirty.

I get to go to the candy store again tomorrow.

I load up into our car and wait for my mother to come out with her steaming coffee. She finally emerges from the front door and makes her way to the car.

"Ready?" she asks as she gets in. She places her mug in the cup holders and shoves the key into the car. The engine makes a low rumbling noise and we are on our way.

"What do you have going on today?" she asks.

"Nothing, I don't think."

"Anything after school? Sports?"

"No."

"Oh."

We sit there in silence because I don't have anything to say and she doesn't have any questions. Eventually, I turn up to the music and change it to my favourite radio station, 96.9 Jack FM. The rest of the drive there I listen to the fast beat of Bon Jovi's 'You Give Love a Bad Name.'

"See you tonight, Addy," my mother says as we pull into the parking lot of the school.

"Yeah, love you," I say, leaning over and giving her a kiss.

"Love you too, sweetie."

I get out of the car and step onto the curb.

"Honey!" my mother calls from the car.

"Yes?" I ask.

"Oh, um nothing."

"Ok."

I walk towards the school and in through the front doors. I have stopped coming early because it's just a waste of time. Karlee is waiting for me inside the doors.

"Hey!" she says as I push open the door.

"Hello," I reply.

"So did anyone ask about yesterday?" she asks as we walk toward room ten.

"Nope, not yet. But I think they know."

"How?" she asks.

"Um... I..." I can't seem to remember what the question was because I am distracted by a sign posted on the wall.

"Adeline? What are you looking at?" Karlee asks me but I can't process the question, it just sounds far away and muffled.

The sign reads: "STUDENT BODY PRESIDENT SIGN UP! ELECTION DAY TOMORROW!"

Maybe if I sign up for student body president this will all end just like it started. Without thinking, I find my hand moving to the pen and signing my name. If there is the slightest chance that I win, maybe it will finish all of this, and I'll become even slightly popular again.

"Student body president? Why?" asks Karlee who has also turned to look at the sign.

"I don't know. Worth a shot," I say.

"Student body president? Why?" asks another person from behind me.

"I thought I just told you," I say turning around but it's not Karlee. "Payton!"

"What makes you think you can win?"

"I don't know," I say, looking at the ground.

"Well, there's no way you're going to win again. Because I'm going to sign up too," say says, grabbing the pen out of my hand and signing her name. Now it's exactly the way it was before.

"Whatever. You will never win. Not again."

She walks away and leaves Karlee and me to ourselves. At least she didn't hit me.

Chapter 27

I am walking into the school like any other day. Everyone is standing around a giant poster hanging on the wall. I push my way through the crowd towards the poster and try to read the poster. In big letters it reads: STUDENT BODY PRESIDENT: PAYTON GRANT.

Everyone around me turns to stare at me. All I can do is stare at the poster. Suddenly, Payton emerges from the crowd.

"I told you, Loser. You can never win again."

"But... but I don't understand," I say.

"You lost," she says and everyone starts laughing.

I run away from all of them, down the hall and into my room. No one chases but I can still hear them laughing in the halls. I can hear Payton shouting out to everybody, "See, that is what you get when you try to do something you shouldn't. People like her are just not meant to be anybody. They're meant to stay at home. Or maybe they should just disappear. Make everything easier."

I slam the door closed and run over to the couch. I never want to feel this way again. I never want to lose - to have everyone stare at me. But most importantly I never want Payton to say I told you so.

Chapter 28

Sunday, Monday. Tuesday, Wednesday. Thursday, Friday, Saturday. Monday, Monday, Monday. Today is Monday again which, to my surprise, I have actually waited all weekend to come. Today is the day of the class election, and everything is exactly the same as it was last time.

We all enter the class and take our seats, as always. Then, Mr. Dunval calls us up alphabetically to check a piece of paper. While the people are voting, we get to read. When my name is called, I walk up and grab the piece of paper from the counter. Obviously I check my own name and then turn back to my seat.

Once everybody finishes, Mr. Dunval announces that he has to go to the office and count the votes from our class, and all the other classes.

The student body president election is different from our class elections because you can only be in grade nine to be elected and everyone in the school has to vote. So that makes it that much more important.

I wait patiently for Mr. Dunval to return with the votes while I read 'The Diary of Anne Frank.' I keep reading while the class all chatters amongst themselves. Lots of people place bets on who they think is going to win and actually, quite a few bet on me.

"Well everybody loves an underdog!" they say.

After I finish three chapters, Mr. Dunval returns and takes his spot at the front of the class to make an announcement. Immediately the class quiets down.

"Ok, class. The winner of the 2014 class election is... Drum roll please."

This comment is met by a round of moans from the class so he just continues.

"Ok, ok. The winner is... Adeline Jamieson!"

Everyone turns to look at me and I don't know how to react. A part of me was hoping to win but I never really thought I could.

"Congratulations Adeline!" he says.

Just as he finishes, the bell rings and everything goes on like before. I move from this class to science and so on for the rest of the morning, until lunch.

—σπεχιαλ—

"Karlee guess what?" I yell at Karlee as she exits room ten.

"I know! I heard! I got all the kids in room ten to vote for you!" she says.

"Do you want to eat outside today to celebrate?"

"No, you know, I'm not feeling very good," she says.

"Are you ok? You don't look so good. Maybe you should just sit down and we can do it tomorrow."

"Ok, I'm sorry I can't celebrate with you."

"That's ok. I think I'm going to go outside anyway."

"Ok. See you soon."

"See ya," I say.

I turn away from Karlee and toward the doors leading to the basketball courts. I push open the small door that's hidden between the lockers and head out toward the basketball courts.

I take a seat inside the key of the basketball court and open up my lunch kit. Today, I have a peanut butter sandwich with extra jam, my favourite, strawberry. I put on extra as a surprise in case I won.

Across the basketball court I can see Elisha and Kaitlyn coming, but no Payton. I know they usually go to the arena for lunch but the arena is the other way. I don't know why they're coming here. One reason I picked this spot is because not a lot of people come here.

"Hey Adeline," they say as they approach me. I close my lunch kit and stand up.

"Hello," I say, uncertain of why they are here.

"So I heard you won the election," says Elisha.

"Yeah," is all I say, still uncertain of their intensions.

"How?" she asks.

"Um… people voted for me."

"Who would vote for you? You're a freak," says Kaitlyn.

Now I know why they are here.

"Well, I guess they just liked me." I say, trying to stay calm.

"Oh, please," she says.

"What do you want?" I ask, a little annoyed.

"Why would you try to get elected again? Don't you remember what happened last time?"

"Look, can you please just go away," I say.

"Why do you think you can talk to us like that?" they say, obviously angry.

"Ok. Look, I understand you're angry."

"No, no we're not angry. We just want you to understand that you will never be able to be president again. Ever. You will always be a loser."

With that, Kaitlyn brings back her hand and punches me in the stomach. I keel over in pain and bring my knees up to my stomach to protect myself from another blow.

"Later, Adeline," they say and walk back towards the school.

I don't want to go back. I don't want to go anywhere. I want to be done. Stop living and this time no song will help me.

"Adeline! Are you Ok?" someone calls from the doors. I can see Karlee standing in the doorways and is making her way towards me. I'm really not in the mood now. All I want to do is leave.

I stand up and run away from the school. I don't know where but just away. I find myself running down the hill and toward the pond. The pond. That's where I'm going to go. To the pond. To the place I love.

Chapter 29

"Adeline! What's going on?" asks Karlee from the road. She still has awhile to go so I just stay where I am.

Somehow I made my way to the pond. I'm just staring at the pond.

"Adeline? What's wrong?" she asks as she crosses the road. I can hear her coughing and she starts to run towards me. Suddenly, she breaks into a coughing fit and falls to the ground.

"Karlee!" I scream, finally breaking out of my trance.

I run towards her and collapse beside her. She isn't breathing I don't think, but I only had two swim lessons before I quit so I only learned a little CPR.

Ok, ok. Think. I need a phone.

I look around and only see one other person sitting on a bench across the pond. I run as fast as I can towards him.

"Sir, can I use your phone please. My friend just passed out and I need to call an ambulance. I know you're not supposed to leave someone alone like that but it was only the two of us. Please?"

"Yeah, yeah," he says, quickly handing me his phone. "Is there anything you need."

I grab the phone and dial 911.

"911, how may we help you?" the girl on the other end of the phone asks.

"Um... Um... I... I forget... No. No. My friend just passed out. She has Down's Syndrome and I don't know what's wrong with her."

"Ok, ok. Calm down, we'll be right there."

I hang up the phone and run back to Karlee. Within minutes the ambulance has arrived, and the siren is wailing loudly.

"Over here!" I yell.

Two men get out of the ambulance and unload a stretcher. They wheel the stretcher over to Karlee and lift her up onto it. I just watch as they do it, they don't even ask me any questions.

"Wait! Wait! Can I come?" I ask as they begin to wheel her away.

"Are you family?" one man asks me.

"No but I am her friend, please?" I ask again.

"Fine," they say.

I hop into the ambulance after they load Karlee in and sit next to her stretcher. I grab her hand and don't let go until we get to the hospital.

The whole ride I just tell her that it will be ok, that there is nothing to worry about, but she doesn't wake up. The heart monitor says she's alive but to me, she's dead to the world.

"Everybody out! We've got to get her in quick!" someone yells from the front.

"Get out kid," says the man beside me.

I scurry out of the back of the truck and wait on the pavement for them to unload Karlee. Without giving me a chance to catch up, they hustle her into the hospital, leaving me in the dust.

I hurry into the hospital after them but once I get there they have already left. I approach the lady at the front desk who looks busy typing on her computer.

"Um... excuse me. My friend just came in here and I was wondering where she went and if I could see her?" I ask her.

"I'm sorry sweetie. That girl just went into the ICU. Only family can see her now."

"Oh, ok. When can I see her?" I ask her. I really want to see her now but I guess that won't work. Besides, it's Karlee that's hurting now so I shouldn't make a scene.

"I'll get her family to let you know. Now go home girl, you don't look very good."

"Oh, ok," I just turn around and walk back. Now that she mentions it, I don't feel good either. I think I'm just going to call my mom and get her to pick me up.

I dial my number once I reach the phone and wait for someone at home to pick up.

"Hello," someone says at the end of the phone.

"Hi mom, I'm at the hospital. Can you pick me up?" I ask.

"What? Why? Are you ok honey?"

"Yeah, yeah, I'm ok. Just come pick me up," I say.

"Ok, I'll be right there," she says and immediately hangs up.

I wait patiently at the front office for my mom to come and when she finally pulls up I couldn't be happier. I just keep rolling everything over in my head. How she fell, how she wouldn't wake up. I've just got to go home and sleep. Just sleep it off.

Chapter 30

What if our roles are reversed.

I am running towards Karlee. She is sitting at the pond, facing the water.

"Karlee! Karlee!" I yell.

I finally reach her and grab for her shoulder.

"What are you doing?" I ask her.

"Go away!" she yells and stands up beside me.

I can feel my heart start to beat faster and faster. I get all sweaty and I can't breathe. She just stares at me. All of a sudden, I feel my feet shoot out from underneath me. I hit the ground hard and just lay there.

I can see Karlee look down at me and scream. She runs around frantically trying to get a phone from someone. I want to get up but I can't. I just lay there with my eyes open. Karlee lays next to me while we wait for the ambulance. She is trying to talk to me but I can't talk back. I want to tell her it will be ok but I can't speak. The ambulance comes and they start to load me onto the stretcher. I really want to get up but I still can't move. They start to load me into the ambulance and Karlee just stands there and watches. Unlike me, she doesn't try to follow me.

Chapter 31

Today I have to go back to school - without Karlee. I don't want to go, not without her. I can't face Payton and Kaitlyn and Elisha again.

But there's nothing I can do. I have to go to school. I can't see Karlee anyway. Besides, there's no way my parents would let me take off school just because I want to.

"Bye mom," I say as I get out of the car.

"Bye honey. Are you sure you're ok?" she asks me.

"Yes mom, I'm fine."

"Ok, see you tonight," she says as I shut the door.

I turn back to the school and brace myself for the day. I push through the doors like I have done so many times before, but this time, it's without Karlee.

That's all I can think about. Without Karlee. I keep my head down and pay no attention to the people around me until one person screams out.

"How could you?!" they say.

I lift my head and am about to ask what they mean when I see the posters. Someone must have followed me to the pond and taken a picture of me and Karlee. In the picture it looks like I'm hitting her but really it was when I was checking for her pulse. Underneath the picture is, in big letters, ADELINE HIT KARLEE. I know exactly who it was too.

I see her walking down the hall towards me and suddenly I am filled with anger and hatred like never before.

"Do you like my posters?" Payton asks as she approaches me.

I just can't handle it anymore. She hates me and Karlee and will do anything to hurt us.

I can't stop it so I bring my arm back and punch her hard in the eye. She falls back in pain and screams out.

"Adeline! My office, now!" says Mr. Stewart, the principal. It's weird how he never notices when it happens to me but he just noticed the one time I did it to her.

I slowly walk past Mr. Stewart and into his office. I have never been in there before. There is a small table in the centre and his desk pushed up against the wall. I take a seat in one of the chairs and wait for him to come in.

When he finally does come in, I sit silently.

"Why Adeline?" he asks me.

"I.." That's as far as I can get. I break down in tears and he just sits there. I can't stop myself from crying. I haven't cried in so long that I just break down under the weight of all that has happened this past week.

"What's wrong Adeline?" he asks me.

"It's just that... I didn't push Karlee. She fell over and now she's sick in the ICU and Payton made these posters that say that I hit her. She's always mean to me and I just can't take it anymore." I say.

"I see. I'll tell you what, you can go back to class and I'll take down all those signs."

"Thank you," I say.

"Actually Adeline, you can just go home. You are looking quite unwell. Maybe when you come back tomorrow you should see Mrs. Greeves," he says.

"Yeah, ok," I say.

I walk out to the phone and call my mom.

"Mom, can you come pick me up? I have to come home," I say.

Without even hesitating she says ok. Maybe everyone thinks I don't look so good.

I grab my stuff and wait at the green cushions in front of the office for my mom. When she finally pulls up I am grateful because I don't think I can handle it any more. I just have to go home, let go.

Chapter 32

I am in a room. The room is dark and cold. I can't see anything. Suddenly, I run at the door and try to break it open.

As if on a CD, voices start to play in my head. They are telling me all the things that are wrong with me. I can't stand it anymore.

The words are pounding in my head and I can't make them go away. I scream and cover my ears. I bang at the walls and scream. The voices are shouting now. Yelling at me, echoing off the walls.

"Help! Help!" I call.

I bang at the door. I start scratching at the door, at the floor, trying to dig a hole under it. Maybe if I can get out of this room I can escape these voices. I scratch and scratch trying to dig through the walls. They suddenly become covered in blood.

Suddenly, a table emerges in the middle of the room. I can't think. The voices are pounding in my head. I approach the table and look at what is on it. A gun. I know exactly what it is for. Relief from the voices in my head.

And

I

wake

up.

Chapter 33

Death is a funny thing. We all die at some point. It could be today, it could be tomorrow, it could be in thirty years. Most people don't control when they die. Everyone has the ability to control how fully they live.

Some people don't want to die but do, and that's sad. Some people want to die and can't. Some people just don't want to go on living. And they don't.

Chapter 34

Today I get to see Karlee. They didn't tell me why because she is still in the ICU, but I don't want to think about it. I think I know but I don't want to.

I brought Karlee some flowers and her favourite book – "The Outsiders" by S. E Hinton. I don't know if she will even know if I am there but I want to see her.

I push open the small door of the hospital and step in.

"Hello! Are you here to see Karlee Jansen?" the girl behind the desk asks me.

"Yeah, can I see her now?" I ask her.

"Oh, honey," she says in a sympathetic voice. "You can go right in."

I don't understand why everyone is talking to me like that. I don't want to understand.

I make my way through the halls of the hospital, following the signs to the ICU wing. When I enter the wing there is a desk at the front with a woman sitting behind it. I approach the desk and wait for her to shift her attention from her screen to me.

"May I help you?" she asks.

"Yes, I am here to visit my friend Karlee Jansen," I reply.

"Ok," she says as she clicks on her key board. "Yes, room 33. She isn't awake yet but you may see her."

"Thank you," I say.

I turn away from the desk and make my way down another series of hallways to room 33. All the doors have blinds on them so you can't see in.

I turn down a corner in the hall and room 33 is right on the wall. Karlee's blinds are down and there is only a small light coming from the door. I slowly push open the door and find Karlee asleep in her bed.

"Karlee?" I ask. Maybe she is awake but just resting.

She doesn't wake up so I walk over to her and brush some loose strands of hair away from her face. I know she isn't going to wake up anytime soon, so I set the flowers down on a small table next to her bed.

I can't stand to look at her anymore. She is dead to the world, she may as well be dead. She is cold and small and I don't want to see her like that. I'll come back tomorrow. Maybe she will wake up.

My mom is waiting for me outside with the car and immediately asks me how Karlee is.

"Ok. She wasn't awake when I went to see her but I think she'll be ok."

"That's good. You know, you should do something nice for her. Maybe make her something, do something for her at school," she says.

Suddenly, I have a great idea. I'm going to make my movie for Karlee. Dedicate it to her.

"Yeah, you're right. I'll think about it."

It takes us about four turns to get home, this time I'm actually paying attention. Last time, I was almost falling over with grief and pain.

When we get home I go straight to my room. I pull out my computer and get to work. Nothing makes me lift my eyes from my computer. I cut and paste and add music and voice-overs. I make it look professional, like a Hollywood movie. I can't do too much though, because I still have some last minute filming that I just thought of.

I spend the rest of the day working on this. I need to get this done... for Karlee.

—σπεχιαλ—

I'm really losing focus, I just don't want to go to school anymore. I've been skipping class every day now, at least one period a day.

Today, I decide to skip fourth period to film. I just film around the school, anybody that I can find in the halls. I hide behind corners and film what people say when they don't think people are watching. I want to show the world what goes on, and that it should stop.

Eventually, the lunch bell rings and I have to go to my room, alone. Lately I have been eating in the closet but I feel like looking through the windows again.

It's really lonely again, it feels just like before. I don't like it. I like having a person around, to be with me. Just when I make a friend, she's taken away. She might not ever come back.

Suddenly, I just can't stand it. I walk to the school phone outside the gym doors. I dial my number and as soon as my mom picks up I ask her to come pick me up.

"Why?" she asks.

"I just can't take it anymore," I say.

After a long pause she agrees. "I'll be there in five minutes."

"Ok," I say and hang up the phone.

I grab my bags from my locker and wait patiently at the couches for my mom to come.

Finally, the doors open and she walks in. I get up and run to her.

"I don't want to do this anymore," I say.

"I know, I know," she says.

"I just want to go home," I say.

"Let's go then."

We walk out to the car and I get in. I sit in the seat and wish I could mould into it. Just melt away and become dust. I came from dust and I will go back to being just that… dust.

We pull up into our driveway and I slowly get out of the car. I grab my bag and wait at the front door for my mom to unlock it. As soon as she does, I drop my bag and go straight to my room.

Without even adding the videos I took today, I click upload to YouTube and collapse on the bed. I just can't take it anymore. There's only so much you can take and I think I have reached the end of my line.

Chapter 35

I am walking through a hallway. I can see a red light at the end. I think it might be a hospital, but for some reason I can hear birds. Everything is hazy and the sounds are muffled. I am being wheeled in on a stretcher. There is a voice coming from behind me but I can't turn my neck to see. We round a corner and there is a field with a pond in the middle.

I get off the stretcher and it disappears. I feel like I am floating towards the centre of the park. I can hear voices behind a tree but can't see who is talking. I reach out and grab for it. When I touch it, it disappears. Behind the tree is Karlee, standing and talking, completely healthy. I am beside her.

"What are you doing here?" I ask her.

"Where, Adeline?" she replies.

"In the park. Why are you here?"

"I'm worried about you. Why did you run away when I called you, Adeline? Do you not like me? Did you not hear me calling for you, Adeline?" Her voice echoes throughout the building.

I just stand there. I can't talk.

"Say something!" I scream at myself.

Karlee continues to speak to me. "Why will you not talk to me Adeline? I am dying! Why won't you talk to me?"

Hearing her say she is dying collapses the shell around me which is not letting me talk.

"You are not dying, Karlee," I say.

"Yes I am Adeline. You have to let me go. You have to forgive and heal and move on."

"No you are not. You are not dying."

She stands there and smiles at me.

"Don't forget to move on. Don't forget about me," she says.

"Karlee listen to me! You are not dying! I can't survive without you! I need you." I say.

"You don't need me anymore. You can stand on your own. Stay true. You shine, Adeline. Don't change yourself to fit in."

"Karlee don't leave me. You are not dying."

"You are right. I am already dead."

I can see her chest moving up and down, faster and faster. She starts to sway back and forth and then collapses to the ground.

"Karlee!" I yell. I try to run towards her but my feet are stuck. I scream. Louder and louder. Louder and louder.

Chapter 36

I wake up, and the sun is shining. Today feels like a good day. Maybe Karlee will wake up today, maybe she can leave the hospital.

I walk over to my computer and check my YouTube. What I see is far more than I'm expecting. Three hundred million views. The comments are rolling in and almost all are angry. They all say "so that's what happens" or "that's so mean!" or "why would they do that?".

Today I have to go to school, but for some reason it doesn't feel like a chore anymore. I want to go to school. I don't feel like it's something that can hurt me. I remember Karlee isn't there, but even that doesn't get me down.

I quickly get dressed and run into the kitchen, doing a cartwheel. I feel light and happy. I feel care-free like my flip can just consume me and take me to a better place. For the first time in a long time, I feel like there is no better place than here.

"Why so happy today?" my father asks from the living room.

"I don't know! I'm just happy!" I reply.

I grab a bowl of yogurt from the fridge and sit at the table.

"What are we watching?" I ask my father.

"'Naked and Afraid' of course," he replies.

I turn my chair so I can enjoy 'Naked and Afraid' while I eat my breakfast.

"Addy, you have to get going to school, are you ready?" my mom yells from her bedroom.

"Yes! I just have to pack my bag!" I reply.

"Ok, I'll be out in a minute. Please do that."

I quickly shove the rest of my yogurt into my mouth and grab my backpack off the table.

"I'm going to the car!" I yell back and leave before I hear a response.

Luckily, the car is always open because my dad has something about locking the doors and forgetting the key so we never lock them.

"Ready?" my mom asks me as she gets into the driver's side.

"Yes," I reply.

That's all I say for the rest of the ride. My mom has been really stressed out lately, so she has been staying home from work a lot. I think she will end up just quitting and being a stay-at-home mom.

"Bye sweetie," she says as we pull up to the school.

"Bye," I say leaning over to give her a kiss.

I get out of the car and walk into school. I just have a feeling that today is going to be a good day, but I don't know why.

—υνιθυε—

Finally it is lunch. Just two periods away from going to see Karlee. I keep having to remind myself not to get my hopes up but I can't help it. While I'm walking to my locker I bump into the new girl, Kassandra.

"Sorry," I say.

"It's ok. I'm Kassandra," she says.

"I'm Adeline," I say, stopping to look at her.

"Do you want to eat with me at lunch?" she asks me.

"Sure," I say. I don't have Karlee to eat with today so I would just be alone anyway.

I walk with her to her locker and then carry on to mine. I put my books away and go back to meet her at her locker.

"At my old school we had to bring our lunch so I'm just getting used to being able to eat at the school," she says.

"Yeah, it takes some getting used to."

We talk all the way to the cafeteria where we get into line. Today they are serving beef on a bun.

"This is my favourite," she says.

"Yeah, I like it too."

After we get our food we sit down at a table and chat all the way through lunch.

Finally, it is the end of the day and I can go to visit Karlee. I make my way to the hospital. This time I didn't bring any flowers but I just have this feeling that she will be awake and we can go pick some in the field instead.

When I reach the hospital I enter through the sliding doors that lead to the main desk. I wait patiently at the counter for the girl to see me.

"How may I help you?" she asks.

"I'm here to see Karlee Jansen again. Is she still in the ICU?" I ask her.

"Um, honey. Karlee Jansen died last night. She had a heart attack. They ran some tests yesterday morning, and found out she had a serious blockage."

My world starts to spin. This can't be happening. We were just going to pick some flowers. She can't be dead. That happy feeling in my stomach that I had three minutes ago is gone. Now I am numb.

I stumble out of the hospital and back onto the street, making my way to my house.

Karlee isn't gone, I keep telling myself.

This isn't happening.

This isn't happening.

This isn't happening.

And then I see her. Standing on the side of the bridge.

Chapter 37

She's standing on the side of the bridge, looking into the water.

"Payton? What are you doing?" I call out to her as I run towards her.

"Leave me alone!" she says.

Finally I have reached her and I grab for her arm.

"Let me go!" she yells.

"No, Payton, I won't."

"Just leave me alone," she screams.

"No come down here," I say.

"No."

I yank on her arm and she falls to the ground. She just lays there and whimpers, crying softly to herself. I don't know what to do so I just stand there.

"You!" she says accusingly, standing up and turning on her heels.

"Me?" I ask, surprised.

"Just let me go! Why can't you just do that?"

"No," that's all I can say.

She stares at me long and hard for a few minutes. I give her my hand and she stands back up.

"Don't you understand? I want to die! Just leave me alone!" she yells.

"I do understand. I do. I wanted to die too, but I can't let you do that," I say.

"Why? Why can't you?"

"Because. I have no one. I understand exactly how you feel. You don't deserve to die. I can't let you die, not like this. You're too young."

"Exactly my point. Do you know what I did to you? I made fun of Karlee and now she is dead! I deserve to die! You should want me to die!"

"But I don't! I want you to live. Forgive and..." And then I think about all the times I had with Karlee and the one message she taught me. We can't forgive and forget. There is no way we can forget what people have done to us or what has happened in our lives. We can't forget but we can heal. We can choose to heal and forgive.

"Forgive and heal." I say as I extend my hand to her. "I can forgive you and I will heal, but you have to do the same for yourself. Forgive yourself for what you've done and heal. I'm willing to if you will. Leave the past in the past." She pauses for a minute and just stares at me.

"I can't,' she says.

"Yes you can," I say, not moving my hand. Finally she grabs it. I pull her in and give her a hug.

"See? You're a good person, you just need to forgive. I forgave you, and you need to forgive yourself."

"Thank you," she whispers in my ear.

"No problem. Now, do you want me to walk you home?"

"Yes. Please," she says.

I follow Payton along the paths to her house. She still lives in the same place she did in grade seven. A small house by Main Street.

The walk there is lovely and full of colour. I especially love the paths to her house. I talk and Payton listens. She is a wreck. She needs someone but I can't be that person. I have forgiven her but I can't forget all the things she did to me. I will heal though. I can forgive her and slowly I will heal.

"Ok, I'll see you tomorrow I guess," I say as we step onto her driveway.

"Do you want to come in?" she asks me.

"No, not today, not right now. I've got to go home," I say, as the reality of what has happened finally sinks in.

"Ok, I'll see you tomorrow Adeline."

"Goodbye Payton."

And that's it. I walk away and back to my house. I have to focus on me now. I have to get home before I collapse. I don't know why I'm taking it so well. I've just got to sleep for a while.

Chapter 38

I can see Payton sitting with Elisha and Kaitlyn. Today will be the first time I'm going to eat in the cafeteria for a long time. But I want to. I'm tired of being alone and I only have myself to blame for that.

I slowly walk towards the table where Payton is sitting. I could sit with Kassandra again but I think I should sit with Payton today.

"Hey," I say as I approach her.

"Oh hi!" she says. "Here, come sit," she says as she shuffles her stuff down and pats a spot on the bench.

I place my lunch down on the bench and sit in the spot that Payton made for me.

"How are you?" I ask her.

"I'm good. Getting better," she says as she smiles at me.

Having me here is really making Elisha and Kaitlyn uncomfortable and I can see it.

"Adeline, I'm really sorry. We all are. I didn't mean for it to go so far. And I'm sorry about Karlee," she says after a while.

"Thanks, but can we not talk about Karlee. I don't think I'm ready yet," I say.

"Yeah, sure. I'm sorry. I didn't realize."

"That's ok," I say looking over at Kaitlyn and Elisha. They are both looking down at their plates.

"We're sorry too," says Elisha. "We didn't mean to hurt you either. We weren't thinking."

"That's ok. Forgive and forget. No, not forget, forgive and heal, " I say looking over at Payton. She smiles and starts eating her chicken strips again.

I suddenly realize what is going to happen. They are going to find out about my movie and they will get angry. It will hurt them again and I don't want to hurt Payton anymore. She's been through so much and I don't know how much more she can take. The best thing for her is to just hear it from me, so that I can apologize and explain to her why I did it.

I stand up and grab my plate from the table.

"What are you doing?" Payton asks.

"I have one more thing to say. Payton, I never meant to hurt you, none of you. I made that video on YouTube. It was wrong of me but I felt like I didn't have a voice and the only way to speak was to show people what was going on. The camera doesn't lie. I never meant to hurt you. I was angry and... and alone. I felt like I didn't have any options left. I'm sorry. I'm sorry." After this I quickly walk away. I can feel them staring at me, shocked and hurt.

Chapter 39

You can only do so much. It has been six months since I talked to Payton that day in the lunch room. Turns out she was more of a wreck than I though. Two months after that, I heard on the news that someone had jumped in front of a transport truck on the highway. It was Payton. Some people just can't live down what has happened, put it in the past and that is what happens. Some things are just out of your control.

Sometimes you have to throw yourself away to start again. Forgive the people who hurt you and apologize to the ones you hurt. For some people, it's hard. They can't let go. Their memories haunt them at night, of what they have done. But it is something they have to do. When you get to that point, you want to start again, you have to let go of the past because if you can't forgive yourself for what you did, you can never start over. You are your own worst enemy.

To hear this happen to a fifteen year old girl is tragic. Fifteen is too young to give up on yourself. You haven't even figured out what you want to do when you grow up. When you grow up things will be better. Some people just don't think things through, about how much everyone around you will hurt if you leave. You may not see it but everyone cares. Everyone.

As for me, I am back to being a straight A student. I am spending all my time making movies, it's what I love to do. I hang out more with Kassandra now. She is a really good artist.

We got a pet dog and I spend the other half of my free time with her. I take my dog, Karlee, for walks around the path, and sometimes go to visit Karlee's (the person's) house.

Sometimes, people come into your life and they fix it without you even knowing. Sometimes, those people are taken away from you, but that just makes you appreciate them more.

The beautiful people are the ones who aren't afraid to be themselves. The beautiful people are the ones who stand up for others; even if they know it will hurt themselves. Those are the beautiful people, the ones we can't understand. The beautiful people who are simple, kind, caring, devoted, inspiring, understanding, compassionate. The ones who change us, who do beautiful things for other people. The beautiful people who are bullied and shot down. The beautiful people who are quiet and listen, waiting for their chance to speak up. Those are the beautiful people, who will always be remembered.

Here's to the beautiful people.

Why I wrote this book

I wrote this book for one of my most funny, creative, and beautiful friends, Emily. She tried to take her life in 2013. I wrote this to tell her that she has to see what is around her. She has to see that no matter what, I am standing behind her. I will support her and help her through this. She has to learn how to forgive and heal and forget.

Emily, try your hardest to forget all that has happened, just block it out and don't let it ever come back into your life. But most importantly, you need to forgive yourself, because I know you haven't done that yet. You have to open your eyes and see the potential you have, you are beautiful and creative. You can take the world if you want it. Your life isn't over until we give up on you, until the world gives up on you. That will never happen. No matter what you do, you can't stop us from loving you, from supporting you. Instead of looking at all your flaws, look at what you are good at. You are amazingly creative, you have the best hair and makeup I've ever seen, but most importantly, you're you. Look at all the things you love, not the things you hate. You love basketball, you love that heavy metal music that I will never get, but you seem to love it. Don't focus on your flaws because you will find some. Everybody will. Focus on the things you're good at and please don't ever give up on yourself. Remember that you are not alone. Find your song, like Adeline. It can even be heavy metal! Always remember that me and Hannah and Karlee and Ariana and Kyra are here to support you. Forever.

Unique does mean weird, but in a good way. One of a kind.

Love Hannah